Barking Up The Wrong Bakery

Christmas

Patti Petrone Miller

Copyright © Patti Petrone Miller 2024

No part of this publication may be reproduced, stored in a retrieval system, or transmitted, in any form or by any means, without the prior permission in writing of the publisher, nor be otherwise circulated in any form of binding or cover other than that in which it is published and without a similar condition including this condition being imposed on the subsequent purchaser.

FBI Anti-Piracy Warning: The unauthorized reproduction or distribution of a copyrighted work is illegal.

Criminal copyright infringement, including infringement without monetary gain, is investigated by the FBI and is punishable by up to five years in federal prison and a fine of $250,000.

Barking Up The Wrong Bakery, Christmas First Edition Copyright © November 2024 by Patti Petrone Miller

Cover art by TMT Book Cover Designs

Published by AP Miller Productions All rights reserved.

Your support of the author's rights is appreciated.

Book List

Barking Up The Wrong Bakery

Accidental Vows
Barking Up The Wrong Bakery, (Christmas)
Barking Up The Wrong Bakery (Thanksgiving)
Best Served Deadly
Bewitching Charms
Hex in the City
Love in Stitches
Mamma Mia It's Murder
Pies and Perps
Sin Takes a Holiday
The Frosted Felony
The Gingerdead Men
The Pendleton Witches
Welcome to Scarecrow Hollow
The Boogeyman

Patti Petrone Miller

Find Patti on Social Media

https://www.facebook.com/pattipetronemiller/

https://www.facebook.com/pattipetronemillerexecutiveproducer/

https://www.facebook.com/elliotandjosephthumbsup/

https://www.facebook.com/halloweenismyfavoriteholiday/

https://www.facebook.com/theholidaysarecoming/

https://www.pinterest.com/pattipetmiller/

Barking Up The Wrong Bakery

Patti Petrone Miller

Barking Up The Wrong Bakery

Chapter 1

The scent of vanilla and butter filled the air as Stephanie Fields whirled around her bakery kitchen, her chestnut hair escaping its messy bun. She hummed "Jingle Bells" under her breath, her hands a blur as she kneaded a mound of snickerdoodle dough.

"Just a few more batches," Stephanie murmured to herself, glancing at the clock. "Then onto the gingerbread house kits."

The bell above the door chimed, and Stephanie's head popped up, a welcoming smile spreading across her flour-dusted cheeks.

"Good morning, Mrs. Hemingway!" she called out, quickly wiping her hands on her apron. "Your cinnamon rolls are fresh out of the oven."

The elderly woman bustled in, her cheeks rosy from the cold. "Oh, Stephanie dear, you're a lifesaver. These rolls are the only thing getting my Harold out of bed these days!"

Stephanie laughed, carefully boxing up the steaming pastries. "Well, we can't have Harold missing out on all the Christmas cheer, can we?" She paused, looking up at Mrs. Hemingway with a twinkle in her eye. "I threw in an extra roll, just don't tell him it's from me."

As she rang up the order, Stephanie couldn't help but notice Mrs. Hemingway's excitement. "You seem extra cheerful today," she remarked.

Mrs. Hemingway beamed. "Oh, it's the grandkids! They're coming for Christmas this year. First time in ages we'll have a full house."

Stephanie's heart warmed at the thought. "That's wonderful! You'll have to bring them by the bakery. I'll have some special treats ready."

As Mrs. Hemingway left, Stephanie turned back to her work, her mind already spinning with ideas for kid-friendly holiday treats. The constant hum of the mixer and the warmth from the ovens wrapped around her like a cozy blanket, reminding her why she loved this time of year so much.

Just then, the bell chimed again. Stephanie looked up to see a young couple, their eyes wide as they took in the festive display cases.

"Welcome to Sugar & Spice!" Stephanie greeted them, brushing a stray lock of hair from her face. "First time here?"

The woman nodded shyly. "We just moved to town. Everyone said we had to try your famous hot chocolate."

Stephanie grinned, already reaching for two mugs. "Well, you've come to the right place. Two peppermint hot chocolates coming right up!" As she prepared the drinks, she chatted with the couple, learning about their move and their plans for the holidays.

"You're going to love Hollybrook at Christmas," she assured them, topping the mugs with a generous swirl of whipped cream. "Make sure you don't miss the tree lighting ceremony next week. It's magical."

As the couple left, clutching their steaming mugs and a box of snowflake-shaped sugar cookies, Stephanie felt a surge of joy. This was why she loved her little bakery so much - the chance to be a part of people's lives, to sweeten their days just a little bit.

With renewed energy, she dove back into her work. Christmas was coming, and there were still so many treats to bake, so much joy to spread. And Stephanie Fields was determined to make this the sweetest holiday season yet.

Stephanie's hands moved with practiced precision as she carefully piped delicate snowflake patterns onto a tray of sugar cookies. Her brow furrowed in concentration, her tongue peeking out slightly from the corner of her mouth. Each swirl and line was executed with meticulous care, transforming the plain cookies into miniature works of art.

"There," she murmured, setting down the piping bag and admiring her handiwork. "Perfect."

Just then, a waft of warm, spicy aroma filled the air, making Stephanie's nose twitch appreciatively. The timer on the oven chimed, and she hurried over, slipping on oven mitts decorated with cheerful gingerbread men.

"Oh, you beauties," she cooed, pulling out a tray of golden-brown gingerbread cookies. The scent of cinnamon, nutmeg, and molasses enveloped her, mingling with the buttery sweetness already permeating the bakery.

As she set the tray on the cooling rack, the bell above the door tinkled. Stephanie looked up to see an elderly couple entering, their cheeks rosy from the cold outside.

"Mr. and Mrs. Winters!" she called out warmly. "Just in time for some fresh gingerbread."

Mrs. Winters inhaled deeply, closing her eyes in bliss. "Oh, Stephanie dear, it smells like Christmas in here."

Stephanie laughed, her eyes crinkling at the corners. "That's the idea! Would you like to try one? They're still warm."

As she carefully wrapped up a selection of cookies for the couple, Stephanie's mind wandered. I hope these bring as much joy to them as Gram's cookies always did for me, she thought, remembering cozy afternoons in her grandmother's kitchen. That's what baking is all about – spreading love, one treat at a time.

The phone rang just as Stephanie was handing the Winters their neatly wrapped package. She flashed them an apologetic smile and reached for the receiver.

"Sugar & Spice Bakery, this is Stephanie speaking. How can I sweeten your day?"

"Stephanie! It's Carol from the Winter Wonderland Festival committee," came an excited voice. "We need a huge favor."

Stephanie's eyes widened as she listened, her free hand unconsciously reaching for a notepad. "Three hundred gingerbread cookies by tomorrow evening? That's quite the order, Carol."

She glanced at her already packed schedule board, her mind racing. How am I going to fit this in? she wondered, biting her lower lip.

"I know it's last minute," Carol continued, "but our usual supplier backed out. You're our only hope for the children's decorating booth!"

Stephanie's resolve softened at the mention of the children. She could almost see their disappointed faces if the booth had to be canceled. "Well, we can't let the little ones down, can we? I'll make it work, Carol. You can count on me."

As she jotted down the details, the bell chimed again. Two more customers walked in, their eyes lighting up at the festive displays. Stephanie waved at them, gesturing that she'd be with them in a moment.

"Thank you, Stephanie! You're a lifesaver," Carol gushed before hanging up.

Stephanie took a deep breath, squaring her shoulders. "Alright, Fields," she muttered to herself, "time to channel your inner Santa's helper."

She turned to greet the new customers, her smile bright despite the whirlwind of tasks now swirling in her mind. "Welcome to Sugar & Spice! What can I bake for you today?"

The bell above the door chimed once more, and Stephanie's eyes lit up as she recognized the familiar figure of Mrs. Hemingway, bundled in a bright red coat and her signature beret.

"Mrs. Hemingway! Right on time for your cinnamon rolls," Stephanie called out cheerfully, wiping her flour-dusted hands on her apron.

The older woman's eyes crinkled with warmth as she approached the counter. "Stephanie, dear, you're a sight for sore eyes. It smells like Christmas in here!"

Stephanie inhaled deeply, savoring the comforting aroma of cinnamon and nutmeg that permeated the air. "That it does. I've just pulled your order from the oven. They're still warm."

As she carefully boxed up the cinnamon rolls, Stephanie couldn't help but notice Mrs. Hemingway's curious glances around the bakery. "Something caught your eye, Mrs. H?"

"Oh, you know me," Mrs. Hemingway chuckled, leaning in conspiratorially. "I was just wondering if you'd heard about the new family that moved in on Maple Street. Quite the excitement for our little town!"

Stephanie raised an eyebrow, a smile playing on her lips. "I hadn't, actually. Been a bit busy here, as you can see." She gestured to the bustling bakery.

Mrs. Hemingway nodded knowingly. "Of course, of course. Well, word has it they've got a handsome son about your age. Single, too!"

Stephanie felt a blush creeping up her cheeks. "Mrs. Hemingway, you're not playing matchmaker again, are you?"

"Me? Never!" Mrs. Hemingway winked, accepting the box of cinnamon rolls. "But a little birdie told me he might be stopping by your bakery soon. Just thought you should know."

As Mrs. Hemingway turned to leave, Stephanie's eyes fell on the covered display she'd been working on earlier. "Oh, Mrs. H! Before you go, would you like a sneak peek at something special?"

Without waiting for a response, Stephanie hurried over to the display, her excitement bubbling over. With a flourish, she pulled off the cloth cover, revealing an intricate gingerbread village. Miniature houses dusted with powdered sugar 'snow', delicate candy cane lampposts, and tiny gingerbread people filled the scene.

"Oh my!" Mrs. Hemingway gasped, her eyes widening. "Stephanie, you've outdone yourself!"

Stephanie beamed with pride, her earlier stress momentarily forgotten. "Do you think the town will like it? I wanted to capture the spirit of Hollybrook at Christmas."

"Like it? They'll love it!" Mrs. Hemingway exclaimed, leaning in to examine the details. "Is that the town square? And look, there's even a tiny version of Sugar & Spice!"

Stephanie nodded enthusiastically. "I stayed up half the night working on it. I can't wait to unveil it at the Christmas Eve Cookie Tasting."

As she gazed at her creation, Stephanie felt a warmth spread through her chest. This is what Christmas is all about, she thought. Bringing joy to others and celebrating our community.

Stephanie stepped out of Sugar & Spice, the little bell above the door jingling merrily behind her. The crisp winter air nipped at her cheeks, a welcome respite from the warm, sugar-scented cocoon of her bakery. She took a deep breath, letting the coolness fill her lungs as she gazed down Hollybrook's main street.

The sight before her made Stephanie's heart swell with joy. Twinkling lights adorned every storefront, casting a magical glow over the snow-dusted sidewalks. Garlands of evergreen swayed gently in the breeze, their rich scent mingling with the aroma of cinnamon and gingerbread wafting from her bakery.

"It's like a winter wonderland," Stephanie murmured to herself, her eyes sparkling as they took in the festive scene. The soft glow of the lights reminded her of fireflies on a summer night, but with a cozy, holiday twist.

Just then, a familiar voice called out, "Hey, sugar plum! Admiring your handiwork?"

Barking Up The Wrong Bakery

Stephanie turned to see her best friend, Samantha Bennett, bounding towards her, blonde curls bouncing with each step. Sam's bright red coat stood out against the snowy backdrop like a cardinal in winter.

"Sam!" Stephanie exclaimed, her face lighting up. "What are you doing here? I thought you were swamped at the gift shop today."

Sam grinned, pulling Stephanie into a warm hug. "I wrapped up early. Thought I'd stop by and see if my favorite baker needed an extra pair of hands. Plus, I couldn't resist the siren call of your gingerbread."

Stephanie laughed, linking her arm through Sam's as they gazed at the twinkling lights. "You're a lifesaver, truly. I could use some help with the Cookie Tasting prep. But first, can we just... soak this in for a moment?"

"Absolutely," Sam agreed, her voice softening. "You know, Em, seeing all this—the lights, the decorations, the way your bakery window glows like a beacon of sugary goodness—it really brings home what makes Hollybrook special. And a lot of that is thanks to you."

Stephanie felt a lump form in her throat, touched by Sam's words. "Oh, Sam. I just do what I love. But having friends like you to share it with? That's what makes it truly magical."

Stephanie wiped her flour-dusted hands on her apron, her brow furrowed in concentration as she piped delicate snowflake designs onto a batch of sugar cookies. The kitchen was a whirlwind of activity, the air thick with the scent of cinnamon and vanilla.

"Sam, could you check on the gingerbread in oven three?" Stephanie called out, her eyes never leaving the intricate pattern she was creating. "I think I smell them, but I can't risk burning these custom orders."

Sam's voice floated back from across the kitchen. "On it, boss! They look perfect, by the way. Golden brown and smelling like Christmas morning."

Stephanie smiled, but the tension in her shoulders remained. "Thanks, Sam. We've got to nail every single treat. The Cookie Tasting is our chance to really wow the town."

As she finished the last snowflake, Stephanie stepped back, scrutinizing her work. Her mind raced with all the tasks still left to do. "I hope these are good enough," she murmured, more to herself than anyone else.

Sam appeared at her side, placing a comforting hand on her shoulder. "Em, they're beautiful. You're being too hard on yourself again."

Stephanie sighed, running a hand through her messy bun. "I know, I know. It's just... this is what I love, you know? I want everything to be perfect."

"Take a break," Sam urged, gently steering Stephanie towards a stool. "You've been at it for hours. How about trying one of those gingerbread men? Quality control, right?"

Stephanie hesitated, then nodded, reaching for a still-warm cookie. As she bit into it, the spicy-sweet flavor flooded her senses. For a moment, the pressure melted away, replaced by pure, simple joy.

"Oh," she breathed, closing her eyes. "That's... that's exactly what I was going for."

Sam grinned. "See? You've got this, Stephanie. Now, enjoy that cookie, and then we'll tackle the rest of your Christmas baking empire together, okay?"

Stephanie nodded, savoring another bite. In that moment, surrounded by the fruits of her labor and the warmth of friendship, she felt a spark of the Christmas magic she'd been too busy to notice.

Stephanie wiped her hands on her flour-dusted apron and stepped back from the counter, her gaze drawn to the bakery's front window. The late afternoon sun cast a warm glow on the display, illuminating the array of festive treats she'd painstakingly arranged earlier.

"Would you look at that," she murmured, a slow smile spreading across her face.

Gingerbread houses with delicate icing icicles stood proudly next to towers of colorful macarons. Intricately decorated sugar cookies shaped like snowflakes and reindeer nestled among pine-scented cupcakes topped with sparkling sugar "snow." The entire display was a winter wonderland in miniature, crafted entirely from sugar, flour, and Stephanie's boundless creativity.

"It's like something out of a storybook," Sam said, coming to stand beside her.

Stephanie nodded, her chest swelling with pride. "I can't believe I made all of this," she said softly. "Sometimes I still feel like that little girl baking with Grandma, you know?"

Sam chuckled. "Well, I'm pretty sure your grandma never made a gingerbread replica of the town square, complete with working fairy lights."

"True," Stephanie laughed, her eyes twinkling. "But she's the one who taught me that baking is about more than just following a recipe. It's about spreading joy."

She turned to face Sam, her excitement bubbling over. "And speaking of spreading joy, can you believe the Christmas Eve Cookie Tasting is just around the corner? I've got so many ideas for new flavors to debut!"

"Let me guess," Sam teased. "Candy cane mocha swirl? Or wait – eggnog snickerdoodle?"

Stephanie playfully swatted his arm. "Hey, don't knock it 'til you've tried it! But seriously, I can't wait to see everyone's faces when they taste these new creations. It's my favorite part of the holidays."

"Well, the whole town is certainly looking forward to it," Sam said. "Mrs. Hemingway was just telling me yesterday how she's already planning her strategy to sample everything without filling up too quickly."

Stephanie's laughter filled the bakery, mingling with the lingering scents of cinnamon and vanilla. "That sounds like Mrs. Hemingway alright. Oh, Sam, I just know this year's event is going to be magical. I can feel it!"

As she gazed back at the window display, Stephanie's mind danced with visions of twinkling lights, the sound of carols, and the warm smiles of her neighbors as they gathered to celebrate the season – all centered around the treats she'd poured her heart into creating.

"You know what?" she said, turning to Sam with a determined gleam in her eye. "I think it's time to start planning the menu. Want to be my taste-tester?"

Stephanie's eyes sparkled with excitement as she reached for her recipe notebook. Just as her fingers brushed the worn leather cover, the bakery phone rang, its shrill tone cutting through the cozy atmosphere.

"Sugar & Spice Bakery, this is Stephanie speaking. How can I sweeten your day?" she answered, her voice warm and inviting.

The smile slowly faded from her face as she listened to the caller. "I see... Yes, of course, I understand the importance. But that's... that's a very tall order for such short notice."

Sam raised an eyebrow, mouthing "What's wrong?" Stephanie held up a finger, signaling him to wait.

"Two hundred gingerbread houses? By tomorrow morning?" Stephanie's voice wavered slightly. "For the children's hospital Christmas party? Oh my..."

She bit her lip, her free hand fidgeting with a stray strand of hair that had escaped her messy bun. The weight of the request settled on her shoulders, threatening to overshadow her earlier excitement.

"I... I'll do my best," Stephanie finally said, her determination breaking through the initial shock. "Yes, I'll make it happen. The children deserve a magical Christmas. Thank you for thinking of us."

As she hung up the phone, Stephanie turned to Sam, her eyes wide with a mix of panic and resolve. "Sam, I think I'm going to need your help. We've got a long night ahead of us."

"What's going on, Em?" Sam asked, concern etched on his face.

Stephanie took a deep breath, the scent of cinnamon and vanilla that usually calmed her now a reminder of the monumental task ahead. "The children's hospital just lost their gingerbread house supplier for their Christmas party tomorrow. They need two hundred houses by 9 AM."

She glanced at the clock on the wall, its steady ticking suddenly sounding more ominous. It was already 6 PM. "I can't let those kids down, Sam. But how on earth are we going to pull this off?"

Chapter 2

The scent of gingerbread wafted through Sugar & Spice Bakery, mingling with the warm, spicy aroma of cinnamon as Stephanie Fields bustled around the kitchen. Her chestnut hair, escaping from its messy bun, tickled her cheek as she bent to slide another tray of Christmas cookies into the oven.

"Oh, sugar!" Stephanie muttered, noticing a smudge of flour on her favorite red and green Christmas sweater. She brushed at it half-heartedly, knowing it was a lost cause. The sweater, like everything else in the bakery, was destined to be dusted with the sweet remnants of her passion.

As she turned to grab her piping bag, her eyes fell on her phone, its screen illuminated with a new email notification. Stephanie's brow furrowed as she recognized the sender: Peter Hamilton.

"What could he want now?" she wondered aloud, wiping her hands on her flour-dusted apron before picking up the device.

Her warm brown eyes widened as she read, her free hand unconsciously moving to cover her mouth in surprise. "Oh my goodness," she breathed, hardly daring to believe the words on the screen.

Stephanie's mind raced as she re-read the email, her heart pounding with a mix of excitement and trepidation. Peter Hamilton, the sharp-suited businessman who'd visited her bakery last month, was offering her an opportunity to expand Sugar & Spice into a franchise.

"Five new locations in the next year," Stephanie murmured, her voice barely above a whisper. "State-of-the-art equipment, marketing support..." She trailed off, her gaze drifting to the worn but well-loved mixer her grandmother had given her when she first opened the bakery.

The ding of the oven timer snapped her back to reality. As she rushed to rescue her gingerbread men from an overly crisp fate, Stephanie's mind whirled with possibilities.

"This could be huge," she said to herself, carefully transferring the cookies to a cooling rack. "But what about the charm of Sugar & Spice? The personal touch?"

She glanced around her cozy kitchen, taking in the twinkling Christmas lights strung along the walls, the handwritten recipes pinned to the corkboard, and the mismatched festive mugs lining the shelves. Each item held a memory, a piece of Hollybrook's heart.

Stephanie sighed, her earlier excitement now tinged with uncertainty. "Oh, Grandma," she said softly to the empty kitchen, "what would you do?"

As if in response, the bell above the bakery door chimed, signaling a customer's arrival. Stephanie straightened her apron, plastered on her warmest smile, and headed out to the front, pushing thoughts of Peter Hamilton's offer to the back of her mind. For now, at least, she had Christmas treats to serve and holiday cheer to spread.

Stephanie's fingers drummed an erratic rhythm on the countertop, her brow furrowed in concentration. She paced back and forth in the bakery, the scent of cinnamon and ginger swirling around her with each step.

"Expansion means more customers, more revenue," she muttered to herself, pausing to adjust a crooked gingerbread house display. "But at what cost?"

She closed her eyes, inhaling deeply. The familiar aromas of Sugar & Spice enveloped her, each scent tied to a cherished memory. Opening them again, she gazed at the wall of photos showcasing smiling faces of regulars who'd become like family.

"This isn't just a bakery," Stephanie said aloud, her voice quavering slightly. "It's the heart of Hollybrook."

The thought of losing that connection made her stomach churn more than any batch of experimental cupcakes ever had. She shook her head, trying to clear the conflicting thoughts.

"Maybe I'm overthinking this," she sighed, reaching for her favorite snowflake-patterned mug. "A cup of peppermint hot chocolate always helps."

As Stephanie busied herself with her comforting concoction, the scene shifted to Hollybrook's main street, where a tall, broad-shouldered figure strolled along the sidewalk.

Jack Carter's piercing blue eyes scanned the quaint storefronts, a small smile playing on his lips. His hands were tucked into the pockets of his wool peacoat, his posture relaxed yet somehow guarded.

"Well, Hollybrook," he murmured, his gaze lingering on a festive window display, "you certainly know how to do Christmas."

The aroma of freshly baked goods wafted through the crisp winter air, catching Jack's attention. His smile widened slightly as he spotted a cheerful sign reading "Sugar & Spice Bakery" just ahead.

"Now that," he said to himself, his voice low and measured, "smells like a story waiting to be told."

As Jack approached Sugar & Spice Bakery, a blur of black fur caught his eye. There, sniffing enthusiastically at the bakery's entrance, was Tessa, her long body wiggling with excitement and stubby tail wagging furiously.

"Tessa?" Jack called softly, his brow furrowing. "What are you doing here, girl?"

At the sound of his voice, Tessa's head whipped around, her expressive eyes widening. She took a hesitant step back, her tail lowering slightly.

Jack crouched down, extending his hand slowly. "It's okay, Tess. It's just me."

The dachshund's nose twitched as she cautiously sniffed his fingers. Jack held his breath, waiting for recognition to dawn in those soulful eyes.

Just then, the bakery door swung open, releasing a heavenly aroma of cinnamon and vanilla. Stephanie emerged, wiping her flour-dusted hands on her festive red and green apron. Her warm brown eyes crinkled at the corners as she smiled at Jack.

"Well, hello there," she said cheerfully. "I see you've met our newest regular customer."

Jack straightened, his reserved demeanor slipping into place like a familiar coat. He hesitated for a moment before returning Stephanie's smile with a small one of his own.

"Jack Carter," he said, extending his hand. "I'm actually dog-sitting this little escape artist for my sister."

Stephanie's eyes lit up with understanding. "Oh! So you're Claire's brother. She mentioned you'd be in town." She glanced down at Tessa, who was now sniffing around Jack's shoes. "This little lady has been brightening up the bakery all week. I think she has a nose for my gingerbread."

Jack chuckled softly, a warmth creeping into his usually guarded expression. "That explains the crumbs I keep finding in her bed. I should have known she had an accomplice."

Stephanie laughed, the sound as warm and inviting as the bakery itself. "Guilty as charged. Though in my defense, who can resist those puppy dog eyes?" She gestured towards the door. "Why don't you both come in? I've just pulled a fresh batch of snickerdoodles from the oven."

Jack hesitated, his hand unconsciously moving to scratch behind Tessa's ears. "I wouldn't want to intrude..."

"Nonsense," Stephanie insisted, her tone brooking no argument. "Any friend of Tessa's is a friend of Sugar & Spice. Besides," she added with a wink, "I could use an impartial taste tester for my new holiday flavor."

As they stepped into the bakery, Jack found himself enveloped in a cocoon of warmth and spice. He breathed deeply, savoring the comforting scents that reminded him of childhood Christmases long past.

"So," Stephanie said, grabbing a plate and piling it high with cookies, "what brings you to our little winter wonderland, Jack?"

Stephanie's eyes sparkled with genuine curiosity as she set the plate of cookies on the counter between them. The snickerdoodles glistened with a dusting of cinnamon sugar, still warm from the oven.

"Can I tempt you with a cookie? Or maybe some hot cocoa to chase away the chill?" she offered, her smile as warm as the treats before them.

Jack's blue eyes flickered with interest, but he shook his head politely. "Thank you, but I'm fine. The aroma alone is... quite something," he admitted, his gaze wandering over the array of holiday treats lining the bakery shelves.

Stephanie nodded, undeterred by his refusal. She could see the curiosity battling with his reserved nature. "Well, the offer stands if you change your mind. Now, about what brings you to Hollybrook..."

Barking Up The Wrong Bakery

Jack cleared his throat, his posture relaxing slightly. "I'm here for the holidays, actually. My sister lives here, but she's away on a business trip. I'm looking after Tessa and her house until she returns."

"Oh, how wonderful!" Stephanie exclaimed, her eyes lighting up. "Hollybrook is magical during Christmas. You picked the perfect time to visit." She paused, tilting her head. "Your sister wouldn't happen to be Sarah Carter, would she? The one who works for that big tech company?"

Jack nodded, surprise evident in his expression. "You know Sarah?"

Stephanie laughed softly. "Small town, remember? Everyone knows everyone here. Plus, Sarah's a regular. She swears by my peppermint mocha cupcakes during the holiday rush."

As they talked, Tessa circled their feet, her nose twitching at the tantalizing scents wafting through the air. Stephanie couldn't help but notice how Jack's demeanor softened when he looked at the little dachshund, a hint of a smile tugging at his lips.

Stephanie's eyes sparkled with an idea. She untied her flour-dusted apron and held it out to Jack. "You know, since you're here, why don't you help me with some holiday baking? I could use an extra pair of hands, and it might be fun."

Jack hesitated, his blue eyes widening slightly. "Oh, I don't know. I'm not much of a baker."

"Nonsense," Stephanie insisted, gently pressing the apron into his hands. "Everyone can bake with the right guidance. Come on, I'll show you the ropes."

Jack glanced down at the apron, then back at Stephanie's warm, inviting smile. Something in her enthusiasm seemed to chip away at his reserved exterior. "Well, alright," he conceded, slipping the apron over his head. "But don't say I didn't warn you."

Stephanie beamed, grabbing a rolling pin from a nearby counter. "That's the spirit! We'll start with something simple. How about some gingerbread cookies?"

As they moved to the work station, Stephanie demonstrated how to knead the dough. Jack watched intently, his brow furrowed in concentration. When it was his turn, he hesitantly placed his hands on the dough, mimicking Stephanie's movements.

"That's it," Stephanie encouraged, her hands ghosting over his to guide him. "Nice and gentle. You've got a natural touch."

Jack's lips quirked into a small smile. "You're just being kind. But I have to admit, this is... oddly relaxing."

As they worked side by side, Stephanie found herself stealing glances at Jack. His initial stiffness had melted away, replaced by a look of quiet contentment. She was about to comment on his progress when a thought struck her, causing her smile to falter.

"You know," she began, her voice hesitant, "I received an interesting offer yesterday. From a businessman named Peter Hamilton."

Jack's eyebrows furrowed slightly, his hands pausing in the dough. "Oh?"

Stephanie nodded, her fingers absently tracing patterns in the flour on the counter. "He wants to invest in the bakery. Expand it, make it part of a chain." She sighed, her conflicted feelings evident in her voice. "It's a great opportunity, but..."

"But you're worried about losing the bakery's charm," Jack finished, his perceptive gaze meeting hers.

"Exactly," Stephanie admitted, surprised by his insight. "This place, it's more than just a business. It's a part of Hollybrook's heart. I don't want to lose that."

Stephanie dusted her hands on her apron, a cloud of flour puffing into the air. "Anyway, enough about my dilStephanies. Let's see how those gingerbread men are coming along."

She reached for the baking sheet, but her elbow caught the edge of a mixing bowl. In a split second, a cascade of sugar rained down, coating them both in a fine, sparkling layer.

"Oh no!" Stephanie gasped, then burst into laughter at the sight of Jack, his dark hair now dusted white, looking utterly bewildered.

Jack blinked, then a slow smile spread across his face. "Well," he said, his blue eyes twinkling, "I suppose this is one way to sweeten the deal."

Stephanie's laughter doubled, and she had to grip the counter to stay upright. "Oh, Jack," she wheezed, "you look like a very distinguished snowman!"

Jack chuckled, the sound warm and rich. "And you," he said, reaching out to brush a bit of sugar from her cheek, "look like you've been caught in a Christmas blizzard."

Barking Up The Wrong Bakery

Their eyes met, and for a moment, the world seemed to stand still. Stephanie felt a flutter in her chest that had nothing to do with the sugar incident.

"So," Jack said, breaking the spell as he began brushing sugar from his shirt, "what's your favorite holiday treat to bake?"

Stephanie smiled, grabbing a broom. "Oh, that's easy. My grandmother's cinnamon star cookies. The smell always reminds me of Christmas mornings as a kid. What about you?"

As they cleaned up and continued baking, sharing stories and laughter, Stephanie couldn't help but feel a warmth that had nothing to do with the ovens. Yet, as the day wound down and Jack prepared to leave, a nagging worry crept back into her mind.

She watched him go, Tessa trotting happily at his heels, and wondered how she could possibly make a decision about the bakery's future. And why did the thought of Jack's opinion on the matter suddenly seem so important?

Stephanie turned back to her kitchen, the scent of gingerbread and possibility hanging in the air. Tomorrow would bring new challenges, but for now, she allowed herself to savor the sweet memory of laughter and sugar-dusted smiles.

Chapter 3

The warmth of the ovens enveloped Stephanie like a cozy blanket as she kneaded a batch of gingerbread dough, her fingers working rhythmically to incorporate the spices. The familiar scents of cinnamon, nutmeg, and molasses danced through the air, mingling with the sugary sweetness of freshly baked cookies cooling on racks nearby.

"Just one more batch," Stephanie murmured to herself, brushing a stray lock of chestnut hair from her forehead with the back of her hand. She glanced at the clock, its festive wreath frame reminding her of the rapidly approaching holiday season. A mix of excitement and anxiety fluttered in her chest.

The cheerful jingle of the bakery's bell caught her attention, and Stephanie looked up, expecting to see Mrs. Henderson picking up her usual order of snickerdoodles. Instead, her gaze fell upon a small, sleek figure darting between the display cases.

"Oh no, not again," Stephanie groaned, recognizing the mischievous dachshund that had been causing chaos in Hollybrook all week. Tessa's nose twitched eagerly as she sniffed the air, her tail wagging with unbridled enthusiasm.

Stephanie wiped her hands on her flour-dusted apron and stepped out from behind the counter. "Now, Miss Tessa," she said in a gentle but firm tone, "you know you're not supposed to be in here."

Tessa's ears perked up at the sound of Stephanie's voice, but her attention remained fixed on a tray of gingerbread men cooling near the edge of the counter. Stephanie couldn't help but chuckle at the pup's single-minded focus.

"I know it smells delicious in here," Stephanie continued, slowly approaching the curious canine, "but we can't have you sampling the merchandise. What would your owner say?"

As if on cue, Tessa let out a small, pleading whine, her big brown eyes gazing up at Stephanie with an irresistible charm. Stephanie felt her resolve wavering, a warmth spreading through her chest despite her best efforts to remain stern.

"Oh, alright," Stephanie sighed, reaching for a small, plain cookie from a nearby jar. "Just this once. But don't tell anyone, okay? It'll be our little secret."

She knelt down, offering the treat to Tessa, who accepted it with gentle enthusiasm. As Stephanie watched the little dog happily munching away, she couldn't help but smile. There was something about Tessa's presence that seemed to melt away some of the stress that had been building up as the holiday rush approached.

"You know," Stephanie mused, giving Tessa a gentle pat, "maybe having a furry friend around isn't such a bad idea after all. But we'll have to find a way to keep you out of trouble."

The sound of the oven timer brought Stephanie back to reality. She stood up, brushing off her knees and heading back to her workstation. "Alright, Tessa," she called over her shoulder, "you can stay for a bit, but behave yourself. I've got cookies to bake and a town full of sweet tooths to satisfy!"

As Stephanie pulled out a tray of perfectly golden gingerbread, she found herself humming a Christmas tune, her earlier anxiety fading into the background. Perhaps this holiday season would bring some unexpected joy after all.

Stephanie's humming was cut short by a familiar scrabbling sound. She whirled around, flour-dusted hands on her hips, to find Tessa once again attempting to scale the counter.

"Oh no, you don't!" Stephanie exclaimed, rushing over to scoop up the determined dachshund. "Didn't we just have a talk about behaving yourself?"

Tessa's tail wagged furiously, her little pink tongue darting out to lick Stephanie's chin. Despite her exasperation, Stephanie couldn't help but chuckle.

"You're incorrigible, you know that?" She set Tessa down near the door, pointing sternly. "Now, out you go. I mean it this time!"

But as soon as Stephanie turned her back, she heard the soft pitter-patter of paws. Glancing over her shoulder, she caught sight of Tessa's sleek black form darting behind a sack of flour.

"For heaven's sake," Stephanie muttered, blowing a stray strand of hair out of her face. "I don't have time for hide-and-seek with a dog!"

Just as she was about to launch into another round of canine cat-and-mouse, the bakery door chimed. Stephanie looked up, her eyes widening as they met a pair of striking blue ones.

A tall, broad-shouldered man stood in the doorway, his dark hair slightly tousled from the chilly wind outside. His gaze, however, wasn't on Stephanie but fixed on a point near her feet. Following his line of sight, Stephanie realized with a start that Tessa had materialized beside her, tail wagging innocently.

"I... uh..." Stephanie stammered, suddenly aware of the flour smudges on her cheeks and the chaos of her usually tidy bakery. "Can I help you?"

The man's eyes snapped up to meet hers, a mix of surprise and something else – was that amusement? – dancing in their depths.

"I think," he said, his voice a rich baritone that sent an unexpected shiver down Stephanie's spine, "the question is whether I can help you."

Jack stepped into the bakery, the warm scent of cinnamon and vanilla enveloping him. He glanced down at Tessa, who was now sitting obediently at his feet, her tail thumping against the hardwood floor.

"I'm so sorry about this," he said, his deep voice tinged with genuine remorse. "Tessa here belongs to my sister. I'm watching her while she's out of town for the holidays."

Stephanie felt a twinge of sympathy despite her frustration. The man's apologetic tone and the sheepish look on his face were disarming. She sighed, brushing a dusting of flour from her apron.

"It's alright," she said, trying to keep the exasperation out of her voice. "But this isn't the first time your furry friend has visited us."

Jack's eyebrows shot up. "Oh?"

Stephanie nodded, gesturing around the bakery. "She's been sneaking in all week. I've lost count of how many times I've had to chase her out."

As if on cue, Tessa let out a small whine, her nose twitching at the enticing aromas filling the air.

"I'm Stephanie, by the way," she added, offering a small smile. "Owner of Sugar & Spice."

"Jack," he replied, returning the smile. "Food critic turned dog-sitter, apparently."

Stephanie couldn't help but chuckle, even as she bent to retrieve a rolling pin Tessa had knocked over earlier. "Well, Jack, your temporary charge has been quite the handful. Just yesterday, she managed to upturn an entire tray of gingerbread men. Do you know how long it takes to decorate those little guys?"

Jack winced, running a hand through his dark hair. "I can only imagine. I'm really sorry about the trouble she's caused."

Stephanie sighed, her gaze softening as she looked at Tessa's hopeful expression. "It's not just the mess, though that's bad enough. It's the constant disruption. Christmas is our busiest time, and I can't afford any setbacks."

She could feel the weight of the season pressing down on her shoulders, the long list of orders and events looming in her mind. How was she going to manage it all?

Jack studied Stephanie's face, noticing the dark circles under her eyes and the tension in her shoulders. He glanced around the bakery, taking in the piles of ingredients and half-finished treats scattered across every surface.

"You know," he said, his voice thoughtful, "I may not be much of a baker, but I do know my way around a kitchen. What if I helped you out for a bit? I could keep an eye on Tessa and lend a hand with your holiday baking."

Stephanie's eyes widened in surprise. The offer was tempting, but years of working solo made her hesitate. "Oh, I couldn't possibly—"

"I insist," Jack interrupted gently. "It's the least I can do after all the trouble Tessa's caused. Besides, it might be fun to see how the magic happens behind the scenes."

Stephanie bit her lip, considering. The warmth of the ovens and the sweet scent of vanilla hung in the air, a reminder of all the work still to be done. She glanced at the clock, its ticking seeming to grow louder with each passing second.

"I don't know," she said slowly, even as exhaustion tugged at her bones. "I'm not really used to having help in the kitchen."

Jack's lips quirked into a half-smile. "Think of it as a temporary partnership. You get an extra set of hands, and I get to keep this little troublemaker out of your hair." He reached down to ruffle Tessa's ears, earning a happy tail wag from the dachshund.

Stephanie's resolve wavered. The idea of sharing her workload, even for a little while, was becoming more appealing by the second. She looked at Jack's earnest expression, then down at Tessa's hopeful eyes, and felt her resistance crumbling.

"Well," she said, a small smile playing on her lips, "I suppose an extra pair of hands couldn't hurt. But are you sure you're up for it? Holiday baking can be pretty intense."

Stephanie took a deep breath, the scent of cinnamon and nutmeg swirling around her. "Alright, Jack," she said, her voice tinged with a mix of relief and apprehension. "You're on. But fair warning: my kitchen, my rules."

Jack's face lit up with a warm smile. "Wouldn't have it any other way, Chef."

Stephanie couldn't help but chuckle at his enthusiasm. "Let's start with something simple. How about we tackle these gingerbread cookies?"

As Stephanie reached for the flour bin, Jack rolled up his sleeves. "Point me in the right direction, and I'm all yours."

They fell into an easy rhythm, Stephanie measuring ingredients with practiced precision while Jack mixed the dough. The soft whir of the mixer blended with the gentle crackling of the oven, creating a soothing symphony of baking sounds.

"You're not half bad at this," Stephanie observed, watching Jack's strong hands knead the dough with surprising gentleness.

Jack grinned, a dusting of flour on his cheek. "I may have picked up a thing or two during my food critic days."

As they worked side by side, Stephanie found herself relaxing. The warmth of the kitchen seemed to wrap around them like a cozy blanket, and the stress that had been knotting her shoulders began to melt away.

"So, what made you leave the big city for Hollybrook?" Stephanie asked, curiosity getting the better of her.

Jack paused, his eyes distant for a moment. "I guess I was looking for something... real. Something that mattered more than the next trendy restaurant or cutting-edge cuisine."

Stephanie nodded, understanding in her eyes. "And did you find it?"

Their gazes met, and Jack's smile softened. "I think I might be getting close."

The timer dinged, breaking the moment. Stephanie turned to the oven, her cheeks flushed from more than just the heat. As she pulled out a tray of perfectly golden gingerbread cookies, she couldn't help but feel that maybe, just maybe, letting someone in wasn't such a bad idea after all.

Stephanie placed the tray of gingerbread cookies on the cooling rack, the spicy-sweet aroma filling the air. She glanced at Jack, who was expertly piping frosting onto a batch of sugar cookies, his brow furrowed in concentration.

"You know," Stephanie said, breaking the comfortable silence, "I never thought I'd say this, but I'm actually glad Tessa decided to cause chaos in my bakery today."

Jack looked up, a surprised smile spreading across his face. "Oh? And why's that?"

Stephanie felt a warmth that had nothing to do with the ovens as she replied, "Because it brought you here. I... I didn't realize how much I needed the help."

Jack set down the piping bag and turned to face her fully. "Stephanie, you've created something amazing here. But even amazing bakers need a hand sometimes."

She nodded, her eyes suspiciously moist. "I've always been so determined to do everything on my own. To prove I could make it work."

"And you have," Jack said softly, reaching out to brush a stray lock of hair from her face. "But you don't have to do it alone anymore."

Stephanie's heart fluttered at his touch. She looked around the bakery, taking in the rows of perfectly decorated cookies, the neatly stacked cake boxes, and the organized chaos that somehow felt more manageable with Jack by her side.

"Thank you," she whispered, meeting his gaze. "For everything."

Jack's blue eyes sparkled with warmth. "Anytime, Stephanie. Now, what do you say we tackle those peppermint swirl cupcakes next?"

Stephanie laughed, feeling lighter than she had in weeks. "Lead the way, Mr. Food Critic. Let's see if you can handle my secret recipe."

As they moved to gather ingredients, their hands brushed, sending a thrill through Stephanie. She realized that in opening her bakery to Jack, she might just be opening her heart as well.

Stephanie's cheeks flushed as she reached for the peppermint extract, the cool glass bottle a welcome distraction from the warmth spreading through her chest. She inhaled deeply, the minty aroma mingling with the lingering scents of cinnamon and ginger in the air.

"You know," she said, glancing at Jack as she measured out the extract, "I never thought I'd be looking forward to the holiday rush quite like this."

Jack raised an eyebrow, a hint of a smile playing at the corners of his mouth. "Oh? And what's different this year?"

Stephanie hesitated, her hand hovering over the mixing bowl. "Well, for one thing, I have an expert taste-tester on hand," she teased, deflecting slightly.

Jack chuckled, the rich sound sending a pleasant shiver down her spine. "Happy to be of service. Though I think my true expertise lies in cleanup duty."

As if on cue, Tessa trotted over, her nails clicking on the tile floor. She sat expectantly at their feet, tail wagging.

"And of course, we can't forget our official crumb collector," Stephanie added, her laughter mingling with Jack's.

She turned back to the batter, folding in the peppermint extract with practiced ease. As she worked, Stephanie found herself stealing glances at Jack, marveling at how naturally he fit into her world. The bakery, usually her solitary domain, felt warmer and more inviting with his presence.

"You know," Stephanie said softly, almost to herself, "I think this might be the best holiday season yet."

Jack's hand brushed against hers as he reached for a spatula, and Stephanie's heart skipped a beat. She looked up, meeting his gaze, and saw her own hope and excitement reflected in his eyes.

"I couldn't agree more," he replied, his voice warm and sincere.

As they continued working side by side, Stephanie felt a newfound sense of optimism blooming in her heart, as sweet and warm as the treats they were creating together.

Chapter 4

The aroma of cinnamon and nutmeg enveloped Stephanie as she kneaded a ball of snickerdoodle dough, her hands working rhythmically. Beside her, Jack expertly piped frosting onto gingerbread men, his brow furrowed in concentration. The bakery hummed with activity as they prepared for the upcoming Christmas Eve Cookie Tasting.

Stephanie snuck a glance at Jack, admiring how quickly he'd picked up decorating techniques. "You're a natural with that piping bag," she said, a hint of playfulness in her voice. "Are you sure you weren't a pastry chef in a past life?"

Jack's lips quirked into a small smile. "Hardly. Though I suppose years of critiquing desserts gave me an eye for detail." He paused, then added softly, "My mother used to let me help frost cookies when I was young. I'd forgotten how therapeutic it can be."

Stephanie's heart warmed at this glimpse into Jack's past. She shaped the dough into perfect spheres, rolling them in cinnamon sugar before placing them on a baking sheet. "My grandmother and I had a tradition of baking snickerdoodles every Christmas Eve," she shared. "The smell always brings me right back to her kitchen."

As she slid the cookies into the oven, Stephanie noticed Jack watching her with curiosity. She tilted her head, prompting him to speak.

"You make it look so effortless," he said, gesturing to the trays of beautifully crafted cookies surrounding them. "I'm beginning to see why your bakery is the heart of Hollybrook's Christmas celebrations."

Stephanie felt a blush creep up her cheeks. "Oh, it's just practice," she demurred. "Though I do have a few tricks up my sleeve. Here, let me show you a shortcut for getting those gingerbread men extra crisp."

She moved closer to Jack, guiding his hand as she demonstrated her technique. The warmth of his arm against hers sent a pleasant tingle through her body. Stephanie pushed the feeling aside, focusing on the task at hand. But as Jack's eyes met hers, full of appreciation and something else she couldn't quite name, she wondered if perhaps the magic of Christmas was working in more ways than one this year.

The cheerful jingle of the bakery's bell cut through the cozy atmosphere, followed by a burst of laughter and the rush of cold air. Stephanie looked up from her work, her face breaking into a wide smile as she saw Samantha and Cindy bustling through the door, their cheeks rosy from the winter chill.

"Reinforcements have arrived!" Samantha announced, her curly blonde hair bouncing as she dramatically swept off her scarf. "We heard there was a Christmas cookie emergency!"

Stephanie wiped her flour-dusted hands on her apron, rushing to greet her friends. "You two are absolute lifesavers," she said, enveloping them both in a warm hug. The scent of pine and peppermint clung to their coats, a reminder of the festive world outside.

Cindy's gentle eyes twinkled as she surveyed the busy bakery. "It smells heavenly in here, Stephanie. Like Christmas came early."

"Well, it's about to get even more festive," Stephanie declared, clapping her hands together. "Sam, I know you've got an eye for design. How about you take charge of decorating? There are some garlands and lights in the back room that need hanging."

Samantha's face lit up. "Say no more! I'll make this place sparkle like the star on top of the Rockefeller Center tree!"

As Samantha bounded off, her enthusiasm infectious, Stephanie turned to Cindy. "And Cindy, I could use your steady hand with some delicate piping work. Think you're up for it?"

Cindy's calm smile was reassuring. "Just point me to the frosting bags, and I'll create some edible masterpieces."

Stephanie felt a wave of gratitude wash over her as she watched her friends dive into their tasks. Jack caught her eye from across the room, giving her a thumbs up as he continued rolling out dough.

"What would I do without you all?" Stephanie mused aloud, her heart full.

"Probably collapse face-first into a bowl of cookie dough," Samantha quipped, already perched precariously on a stepladder, tinsel draped around her neck like a glittery boa.

The bakery filled with the sound of laughter, the warmth of friendship, and the promise of a truly magical Christmas Eve celebration. As Stephanie returned to her workstation, she couldn't help but feel that with her friends by her side, anything was possible.

The aroma of cinnamon and ginger wafted through the air as Stephanie and Jack stood side by side at the large wooden worktable, carefully assembling the intricate gingerbread house that would serve as the centerpiece for the Christmas Eve Cookie Tasting event. Stephanie's nimble fingers delicately piped royal icing along the edges of a gingerbread wall, her brow furrowed in concentration.

"You know," Jack said, his voice low and thoughtful as he held two pieces together, waiting for the icing to set, "I never thought I'd find myself enjoying something as quaint as building a gingerbread house."

Stephanie glanced up at him, a smile tugging at the corners of her lips. "Oh? And what does the esteemed food critic usually do during the holiday season? Attend fancy galas and sample canapés?"

Jack chuckled, the sound warm and rich. "Something like that. But this... this feels more real somehow."

As they worked, Stephanie couldn't help but notice how Jack's strong hands, once used to wield a critic's pen, now carefully placed candy canes along the roofline of their creation. The juxtaposition made her heart flutter.

"So, what's your vision for the event?" Stephanie asked, reaching for a bag of gumdrops. "I'm thinking we could transform the bakery into a winter wonderland."

Jack's blue eyes lit up with interest. "I like that idea. Maybe we could create little vignettes around the room? Like miniature Christmas scenes with the different cookie displays as the centerpieces."

Stephanie's mind raced with possibilities. "Oh! We could have a North Pole station with peppermint cookies, and a cozy fireplace setup with gingerbread men!"

"And don't forget a Christmas tree corner with those star-shaped sugar cookies you make," Jack added, a hint of admiration in his voice.

As they continued to brainstorm, Stephanie felt a warmth spreading through her chest that had nothing to do with the heat from the ovens. Jack's enthusiasm and creativity surprised and delighted her. She found herself imagining what it would be like to have him by her side not just for this event, but for all the Christmases to come.

"You know," Stephanie said softly, placing a tiny fondant wreath on the gingerbread house's door, "I think this event might just be our best one yet."

Jack's hand brushed against hers as he reached for the piping bag, sending a jolt of electricity through her. "With you at the helm, Stephanie, I have no doubt it will be nothing short of magical."

Stephanie felt a blush creep up her cheeks at Jack's compliment. She cleared her throat, trying to regain her composure. "Well, there's only one way to find out if our creations are as magical as we hope. Taste test time!"

Jack's expression sparkled with mischief. "Is that a challenge I hear, Ms. Fields?"

"You bet it is, Mr. Carter," Stephanie replied, her competitive spirit rising to the surface. She grabbed a platter of assorted cookies and placed it on the counter between them. "May the best baker win!"

The rich aroma of butter, sugar, and spices filled the air as Stephanie selected a snowflake-shaped sugar cookie, dusted with a light shimmer of

edible glitter. She took a bite, savoring the delicate vanilla flavor and the satisfying crunch.

"Mmm," she hummed appreciatively. "The texture is perfect. Your turn, Jack."

Jack chose a chocolate crinkle cookie, its dark surface cracked to reveal a fudgy interior. He took a generous bite, closing his eyes as he chewed thoughtfully.

"The balance of chocolate and sweetness is spot on," he declared, licking a spot of powdered sugar from his lip.

Stephanie tried not to stare, her heart fluttering at the sight. She was about to reach for another cookie when Sam's voice rang out from the doorway.

"Cookie tasting? Count us in!" Sam bounded into the kitchen, Cindy close behind.

"Perfect timing," Stephanie laughed. "We need some impartial judges for our little competition."

Barking Up The Wrong Bakery

Cindy's expression widened with delight. "Ooh, a bake-off between Stephanie and Jack? This I've got to see!"

As Sam and Cindy settled in, Stephanie couldn't help but feel a surge of joy. The kitchen was filled with laughter, the sweet scent of baked goods, and the warmth of friendship. She caught Jack's eye and saw her own happiness reflected there. Whatever the outcome of their playful competition, Stephanie knew that this moment was already a winner in her book.

Stephanie stepped back, her eyes widening as she took in the transformed bakery. The warm glow of twinkling lights reflected off the polished display cases, casting a magical shimmer across the room. Garlands of fresh pine and cinnamon sticks adorned the walls, filling the air with a spicy-sweet aroma that mingled with the rich scent of freshly baked cookies.

"Oh my goodness," she breathed, her hand instinctively reaching for Jack's arm. "It's like a winter wonderland in here!"

Jack's lips curved into a soft smile as he surveyed their handiwork. "It really came together, didn't it?"

Sam bounced on her toes, her curls bobbing with excitement. "The gingerbread village looks amazing, Stephanie! I can't believe you and Jack made that in one afternoon."

"Well, we had some pretty fantastic helpers," Stephanie replied, giving Sam and Cindy a warm smile. Her gaze drifted to the intricate gingerbread centerpiece, marveling at the delicate icing that Jack had piped onto the miniature houses. "I couldn't have done any of this without you all."

Cindy beamed, adjusting a string of lights. "It was our pleasure. This place is going to knock everyone's socks off tomorrow!"

As they began to tidy up, Stephanie found herself stealing glances at Jack. He moved with quiet efficiency, his strong hands gentle as he wrapped leftover cookies in wax paper. She couldn't help but wonder what those hands would feel like intertwined with her own.

Shaking off the thought, Stephanie focused on wiping down the counters. "I can't thank you all enough for today," she said, her voice thick with emotion. "This event means so much to me, and having your support... well, it's the best Christmas gift I could ask for."

Jack paused in his task, his gaze meeting hers with an intensity that made her breath catch. "We're happy to help, Stephanie. You've created something special here."

"He's right," Sam chimed in, slinging an arm around Stephanie's shoulders. "Sugar & Spice is the heart of Hollybrook, and you're the one who keeps it beating."

Stephanie felt warmth bloom in her chest, overwhelmed by the love and support surrounding her. As they finished cleaning, the bakery filled with laughter and the gentle clinking of utensils being put away, she knew that no matter what challenges lay ahead, she had found her own little Christmas miracle right here.

Stephanie's excitement grew with inspiration as she hung up her flour-dusted apron. "You know what? We deserve to celebrate," she announced, her voice filled with warmth. "How about we head over to The Cozy Kettle for dinner? My treat!"

Sam let out an enthusiastic whoop. "Now you're talking! I've been dreaming about their famous pot pie all day."

Jack's lips curved into a soft smile. "That sounds perfect," he agreed, his deep voice sending a pleasant shiver down Stephanie's spine.

Cindy clapped her hands together. "Oh, I love The Cozy Kettle! Their hot cocoa is to die for."

As they bundled up in their winter coats, Stephanie couldn't help but feel a surge of joy. The bakery, now quiet and filled with the lingering scent of cinnamon and vanilla, had witnessed so much laughter and camaraderie today. She hoped the evening ahead would bring even more.

"Ready to brave the cold?" Jack asked, holding the door open. His blue eyes twinkled with amusement.

Stephanie stepped out into the crisp winter air, snowflakes immediately dancing around her. "After today's baking marathon, I think we could all use a little cool down," she quipped.

The street was aglow with twinkling Christmas lights, casting a warm glow on the fresh snow. As they walked, their breath visible in the chilly air, Stephanie found herself falling into step beside Jack.

"So, city boy," she teased gently, "how are you liking small-town life so far?"

Jack chuckled, a rich sound that made Stephanie's heart skip a beat. "It's growing on me," he admitted. "Especially the company."

Barking Up The Wrong Bakery

Ahead of them, Sam and Cindy were engaged in an animated conversation about holiday traditions. Their laughter echoed through the quiet street, punctuated by the distant sound of carolers.

Stephanie felt a warmth that had nothing to do with her cozy sweater. As they approached The Cozy Kettle, its windows glowing invitingly, she knew that this night – surrounded by friends both old and new – was exactly what she needed to make this Christmas truly magical.

Chapter 5

The aroma of cinnamon and nutmeg enveloped Stephanie as she kneaded a ball of snickerdoodle dough, her hands working rhythmically. Beside her, Jack expertly piped frosting onto gingerbread men, his brow furrowed in concentration. The bakery hummed with activity as they prepared for the upcoming Christmas Eve Cookie Tasting.

Stephanie snuck a glance at Jack, admiring how quickly he'd picked up decorating techniques. "You're a natural with that piping bag," she said, a hint of playfulness in her voice. "Are you sure you weren't a pastry chef in a past life?"

Jack's lips quirked into a small smile. "Hardly. Though I suppose years of critiquing desserts gave me an eye for detail." He paused, then added softly, "My mother used to let me help frost cookies when I was young. I'd forgotten how therapeutic it can be."

Stephanie's heart warmed at this glimpse into Jack's past. She shaped the dough into perfect spheres, rolling them in cinnamon sugar before placing them on a baking sheet. "My grandmother and I had a tradition of baking snickerdoodles every Christmas Eve," she shared. "The smell always brings me right back to her kitchen."

As she slid the cookies into the oven, Stephanie noticed Jack watching her with curiosity. She tilted her head, prompting him to speak.

"You make it look so effortless," he said, gesturing to the trays of beautifully crafted cookies surrounding them. "I'm beginning to see why your bakery is the heart of Hollybrook's Christmas celebrations."

Stephanie felt a blush creep up her cheeks. "Oh, it's just practice," she demurred. "Though I do have a few tricks up my sleeve. Here, let me show you a shortcut for getting those gingerbread men extra crisp."

Barking Up The Wrong Bakery

She moved closer to Jack, guiding his hand as she demonstrated her technique. The warmth of his arm against hers sent a pleasant tingle through her body. Stephanie pushed the feeling aside, focusing on the task at hand. But as Jack's eyes met hers, full of appreciation and something else she couldn't quite name, she wondered if perhaps the magic of Christmas was working in more ways than one this year.

The cheerful jingle of the bakery's bell cut through the cozy atmosphere, followed by a burst of laughter and the rush of cold air. Stephanie looked up from her work, her face breaking into a wide smile as she saw Samantha and Cindy bustling through the door, their cheeks rosy from the winter chill.

"Reinforcements have arrived!" Samantha announced, her curly blonde hair bouncing as she dramatically swept off her scarf. "We heard there was a Christmas cookie emergency!"

Stephanie wiped her flour-dusted hands on her apron, rushing to greet her friends. "You two are absolute lifesavers," she said, enveloping them both in a warm hug. The scent of pine and peppermint clung to their coats, a reminder of the festive world outside.

Cindy's gentle eyes twinkled as she surveyed the busy bakery. "It smells heavenly in here, Stephanie. Like Christmas came early."

"Well, it's about to get even more festive," Stephanie declared, clapping her hands together. "Sam, I know you've got an eye for design. How about you take charge of decorating? There are some garlands and lights in the back room that need hanging."

Samantha's face lit up. "Say no more! I'll make this place sparkle like the star on top of the Rockefeller Center tree!"

As Samantha bounded off, her enthusiasm infectious, Stephanie turned to Cindy. "And Cindy, I could use your steady hand with some delicate piping work. Think you're up for it?"

Cindy's calm smile was reassuring. "Just point me to the frosting bags, and I'll create some edible masterpieces."

Stephanie felt a wave of gratitude wash over her as she watched her friends dive into their tasks. Jack caught her eye from across the room, giving her a thumbs up as he continued rolling out dough.

"What would I do without you all?" Stephanie mused aloud, her heart full.

"Probably collapse face-first into a bowl of cookie dough," Samantha quipped, already perched precariously on a stepladder, tinsel draped around her neck like a glittery boa.

The bakery filled with the sound of laughter, the warmth of friendship, and the promise of a truly magical Christmas Eve celebration. As Stephanie returned to her workstation, she couldn't help but feel that with her friends by her side, anything was possible.

The aroma of cinnamon and ginger wafted through the air as Stephanie and Jack stood side by side at the large wooden worktable, carefully assembling the intricate gingerbread house that would serve as the centerpiece for the Christmas Eve Cookie Tasting event. Stephanie's nimble fingers delicately piped royal icing along the edges of a gingerbread wall, her brow furrowed in concentration.

"You know," Jack said, his voice low and thoughtful as he held two pieces together, waiting for the icing to set, "I never thought I'd find myself enjoying something as quaint as building a gingerbread house."

Stephanie glanced up at him, a smile tugging at the corners of her lips. "Oh? And what does the esteemed food critic usually do during the holiday season? Attend fancy galas and sample canapés?"

Jack chuckled, the sound warm and rich. "Something like that. But this... this feels more real somehow."

As they worked, Stephanie couldn't help but notice how Jack's strong hands, once used to wield a critic's pen, now carefully placed candy canes along the roofline of their creation. The juxtaposition made her heart flutter.

"So, what's your vision for the event?" Stephanie asked, reaching for a bag of gumdrops. "I'm thinking we could transform the bakery into a winter wonderland."

Jack lit up with interest. "I like that idea. Maybe we could create little vignettes around the room? Like miniature Christmas scenes with the different cookie displays as the centerpieces."

Stephanie's mind raced with possibilities. "Oh! We could have a North Pole station with peppermint cookies, and a cozy fireplace setup with gingerbread men!"

"And don't forget a Christmas tree corner with those star-shaped sugar cookies you make," Jack added, a hint of admiration in his voice.

As they continued to brainstorm, Stephanie felt a warmth spreading through her chest that had nothing to do with the heat from the

Barking Up The Wrong Bakery

ovens. Jack's enthusiasm and creativity surprised and delighted her. She found herself imagining what it would be like to have him by her side not just for this event, but for all the Christmases to come.

"You know," Stephanie said softly, placing a tiny fondant wreath on the gingerbread house's door, "I think this event might just be our best one yet."

Jack's hand brushed against hers as he reached for the piping bag, sending a jolt of electricity through her. "With you at the helm, Stephanie, I have no doubt it will be nothing short of magical."

Stephanie felt a blush creep up her cheeks at Jack's compliment. She cleared her throat, trying to regain her composure. "Well, there's only one way to find out if our creations are as magical as we hope. Taste test time!"

Jack's eyes sparkled with mischief. "Is that a challenge I hear, Ms. Fields?"

"You bet it is, Mr. Carter," Stephanie replied, her competitive spirit rising to the surface. She grabbed a platter of assorted cookies and placed it on the counter between them. "May the best baker win!"

The rich aroma of butter, sugar, and spices filled the air as Stephanie selected a snowflake-shaped sugar cookie, dusted with a light shimmer of edible glitter. She took a bite, savoring the delicate vanilla flavor and the satisfying crunch.

"Mmm," she hummed appreciatively. "The texture is perfect. Your turn, Jack."

Jack chose a chocolate crinkle cookie, its dark surface cracked to reveal a fudgy interior. He took a generous bite, closing his eyes as he chewed thoughtfully.

"The balance of chocolate and sweetness is spot on," he declared, licking a spot of powdered sugar from his lip.

Stephanie tried not to stare, her heart fluttering at the sight. She was about to reach for another cookie when Sam's voice rang out from the doorway.

"Cookie tasting? Count us in!" Sam bounded into the kitchen, Cindy close behind.

"Perfect timing," Stephanie laughed. "We need some impartial judges for our little competition."

Cindy's eyes widened with delight. "Ooh, a bake-off between Stephanie and Jack? This I've got to see!"

As Sam and Cindy settled in, Stephanie couldn't help but feel a surge of joy. The kitchen was filled with laughter, the sweet scent of baked goods, and the warmth of friendship. She caught Jack's eye and saw her own happiness reflected there. Whatever the outcome of their playful competition, Stephanie knew that this moment was already a winner in her book.

Stephanie stepped back, her eyes widening as she took in the transformed bakery. The warm glow of twinkling lights reflected off the polished display cases, casting a magical shimmer across the room. Garlands of fresh pine and cinnamon sticks adorned the walls, filling the air with a spicy-sweet aroma that mingled with the rich scent of freshly baked cookies.

"Oh my goodness," she breathed, her hand instinctively reaching for Jack's arm. "It's like a winter wonderland in here!"

Jack's lips curved into a soft smile as he surveyed their handiwork. "It really came together, didn't it?"

Sam bounced on her toes, her curls bobbing with excitement. "The gingerbread village looks amazing, Stephanie! I can't believe you and Jack made that in one afternoon."

"Well, we had some pretty fantastic helpers," Stephanie replied, giving Sam and Cindy a warm smile. Her gaze drifted to the intricate gingerbread centerpiece, marveling at the delicate icing that Jack had piped onto the miniature houses. "I couldn't have done any of this without you all."

Cindy beamed, adjusting a string of lights. "It was our pleasure. This place is going to knock everyone's socks off tomorrow!"

As they began to tidy up, Stephanie found herself stealing glances at Jack. He moved with quiet efficiency, his strong hands gentle as he wrapped leftover cookies in wax paper. She couldn't help but wonder what those hands would feel like intertwined with her own.

Shaking off the thought, Stephanie focused on wiping down the counters. "I can't thank you all enough for today," she said, her voice thick with emotion. "This event means so much to me, and having your support... well, it's the best Christmas gift I could ask for."

Jack paused in his task, his gaze meeting hers with an intensity that made her breath catch. "We're happy to help, Stephanie. You've created something special here."

"He's right," Sam chimed in, slinging an arm around Stephanie's shoulders. "Sugar & Spice is the heart of Hollybrook, and you're the one who keeps it beating."

Stephanie felt warmth bloom in her chest, overwhelmed by the love and support surrounding her. As they finished cleaning, the bakery filled with laughter and the gentle clinking of utensils being put away, she knew that no matter what challenges lay ahead, she had found her own little Christmas miracle right here.

Stephanie's excitement grew with inspiration as she hung up her flour-dusted apron. "You know what? We deserve to celebrate," she announced, her voice filled with warmth. "How about we head over to The Cozy Kettle for dinner? My treat!"

Sam let out an enthusiastic whoop. "Now you're talking! I've been dreaming about their famous pot pie all day."

Jack's lips curved into a soft smile. "That sounds perfect," he agreed, his deep voice sending a pleasant shiver down Stephanie's spine.

Cindy clapped her hands together. "Oh, I love The Cozy Kettle! Their hot cocoa is to die for."

As they bundled up in their winter coats, Stephanie couldn't help but feel a surge of joy. The bakery, now quiet and filled with the lingering scent of cinnamon and vanilla, had witnessed so much laughter and camaraderie today. She hoped the evening ahead would bring even more.

"Ready to brave the cold?" Jack asked, holding the door open. His blue eyes twinkled with amusement.

Stephanie stepped out into the crisp winter air, snowflakes immediately dancing around her. "After today's baking marathon, I think we could all use a little cool down," she quipped.

The street was aglow with twinkling Christmas lights, casting a warm glow on the fresh snow. As they walked, their breath visible in the chilly air, Stephanie found herself falling into step beside Jack.

"So, city boy," she teased gently, "how are you liking small-town life so far?"

Jack chuckled, a rich sound that made Stephanie's heart skip a beat. "It's growing on me," he admitted. "Especially the company."

Ahead of them, Sam and Cindy were engaged in an animated conversation about holiday traditions. Their laughter echoed through the quiet street, punctuated by the distant sound of carolers.

Stephanie felt a warmth that had nothing to do with her cozy sweater. As they approached The Cozy Kettle, its windows glowing invitingly, she knew that this night – surrounded by friends both old and new – was exactly what she needed to make this Christmas truly magical.

Chapter 6

Stephanie's heart fluttered as she turned to Jack, her chestnut hair escaping its messy bun in wisps around her face. "So, what do you say we take a little tour of Hollybrook's Christmas wonderland?" She gestured towards the town square with a flour-dusted hand. "I promise it'll put even the Grinch in the holiday spirit."

Jack's piercing blue eyes crinkled at the corners, a hint of a smile playing on his lips. "Well, as a former New Yorker, I consider myself something of a Christmas cynic. But I'm willing to be converted."

"Challenge accepted," Stephanie grinned, looping her arm through his. The warmth of his body seeped through her cozy sweater, sending a shiver down her spine that had nothing to do with the crisp December air.

As they strolled into the square, Stephanie felt a childlike wonder wash over her. Twinkling lights draped every tree like a cascade of stars, transforming the familiar space into a glittering fairyland. The scent of pine and cinnamon wafted on the breeze, mingling with the sweet aroma of candied almonds from a nearby vendor.

"It's like stepping into a snow globe," Jack murmured, his deep voice tinged with awe.

Stephanie glanced up at him, drinking in the way the soft light illuminated his strong features. *He looks softer here,* she thought, *less like the aloof food critic and more like a man rediscovering the magic of the season.*

"Wait until you see the giant gingerbread house," she said, tugging him gently towards the center of the square. "I may have had a hand in its construction."

Jack raised an eyebrow. "Let me guess – you're responsible for the structurally sound roof and perfectly aligned candy canes?"

Stephanie laughed, the sound carrying on the crisp air. "You know me too well already. Though I can't take credit for the gumdrop walkway – that was all Mrs. Henderson from the craft store."

As they wandered past glittering snowflake sculptures and towering nutcrackers, Stephanie found herself sneaking glances at Jack. His earlier reservations seemed to melt away with each step, replaced by a quiet wonder that made her heart swell.

I wonder if he can feel it too, she mused. This connection, this sense that maybe, just maybe, we were meant to find each other in this little corner of Christmas magic.

The melodious strains of "Silent Night" drifted through the air, drawing Stephanie's attention. She tugged gently on Jack's arm, her eyes sparkling with excitement.

"Oh, listen! The Hollybrook Harmonies are performing tonight," she exclaimed, gesturing towards a group of carolers gathered near the town's ancient oak tree. Their voices blended in perfect harmony, creating a tapestry of sound that seemed to wrap around them like a warm blanket.

Jack tilted his head, a soft smile playing on his lips. "They're quite good," he murmured, his breath visible in the chilly air. "I haven't heard carolers like this since I was a kid."

Stephanie's heart warmed at the wistful note in his voice. "They practice all year for the holiday season," she explained, unconsciously leaning closer to him. "Mrs. Willoughby – the one in the red scarf – she used to be on Broadway, you know."

As they stood there, letting the music wash over them, Stephanie found herself humming along softly. She caught Jack watching her, an unreadable expression in his eyes.

"What?" she asked, suddenly self-conscious.

He shook his head, still smiling. "Nothing. It's just... nice to see someone so genuinely in love with Christmas."

Stephanie felt a blush creep up her cheeks, and not just from the cold. "Well, shall we continue our tour? There's so much more to see."

Barking Up The Wrong Bakery

They strolled arm in arm down Main Street, passing by shop windows that glowed with warmth and holiday cheer. Stephanie's eyes darted from one display to the next, each one a familiar delight.

"Look at Mr. Peterson's toy shop," she said, pointing to a whimsical scene of mechanical elves busily wrapping presents. "He changes the display every week. The kids in town love to guess what it'll be next."

Jack leaned in closer to peer at the intricate details. "It's incredible," he admitted. "I've never seen anything quite like it."

As they continued their walk, Stephanie found herself stealing glances at Jack's profile, illuminated by the twinkling lights. She couldn't help but wonder what other hidden depths lay beneath his polished exterior.

Maybe, just maybe, she thought, this Christmas will bring more than just the usual holiday magic.

As they rounded the corner, a rich, nutty aroma wafted through the air, instantly catching Stephanie's attention. Her eyes lit up, and she tugged gently on Jack's arm.

"Oh! Do you smell that?" she asked, her voice filled with excitement. "It's Mr. Wilkins and his famous roasted chestnuts. We absolutely have to try some!"

Jack inhaled deeply, a smile spreading across his face. "It does smell incredible," he agreed. "Lead the way, Christmas expert."

Stephanie laughed, the sound as warm and inviting as the scent drawing them closer. She guided Jack towards a quaint wooden cart, where an elderly man in a red and green striped scarf was tending to a small fire.

"Evening, Mr. Wilkins!" Stephanie called out cheerfully. "Two bags of your finest chestnuts, please."

The vendor looked up, his weathered face breaking into a wide grin. "Well, if it isn't our very own Sugar Plum Fairy! Showing our visitor the best of Hollybrook, are we?"

Stephanie felt a blush creep up her cheeks. "Jack, this is Mr. Wilkins. He's been roasting chestnuts here longer than I've been alive."

"A pleasure," Jack said, extending his hand.

As Mr. Wilkins prepared their treats, Stephanie found herself unconsciously leaning closer to Jack, savoring the warmth radiating from him in the chilly evening air.

"Here you are," Mr. Wilkins said, handing over two paper bags. "Enjoy, you two!"

Stephanie reached for her wallet, but Jack beat her to it. "My treat," he insisted, passing over a few bills.

"Thank you," Stephanie said softly, touched by the gesture.

As they walked away, hands clasped around warm bags of chestnuts, Stephanie couldn't help but feel a flutter in her stomach that had nothing to do with the anticipation of the treat.

"So," Jack said, carefully peeling open a chestnut, "what's the verdict? Do these live up to the hype?"

Stephanie popped a chestnut into her mouth, savoring the rich, buttery flavor. "Mmm," she hummed contentedly. "Even better than I remembered. Here, you have to try one!"

Without thinking, she held out a perfectly roasted chestnut to Jack's lips. He hesitated for a moment before accepting it, his eyes never leaving hers as he took a bite.

"Delicious," he murmured, and Stephanie wasn't sure if he was talking about the chestnut or something else entirely.

Stephanie's tugged gently on Jack's hand, leading him towards a small park nestled between snow-dusted evergreens. The sound of laughter and the scrape of blades on ice grew louder with each step.

"I hope you brought your balance," Stephanie teased, gesturing towards the makeshift ice rink that had transformed the park's central pond into a winter wonderland. Strings of twinkling lights crisscrossed overhead, casting a warm glow on the scene below.

Jack's eyebrows shot up. "Ice skating? I don't know, Stephanie. It's been years since I've been on the ice."

Stephanie squeezed his hand reassuringly. "Don't worry, I'll make sure you don't fall. Besides, what's Christmas without a little adventure?"

As they approached the rink's edge, Stephanie couldn't help but notice how the fairy lights reflected in Jack's blue eyes, making them shine with an almost magical quality. She felt a flutter in her chest that had nothing to do with the cold.

"Alright," Jack conceded with a chuckle. "But fair warning - I may not be as graceful as those food critics you saw on TV."

They laced up their rental skates, the leather stiff and cold against Stephanie's ankles. She stood first, offering her hand to Jack. "Ready?"

He took it, his larger hand enveloping hers. "As I'll ever be."

Barking Up The Wrong Bakery

They glided onto the ice, Stephanie moving with practiced ease while Jack's movements were more tentative. She kept a firm grip on his hand, guiding him as they slowly circled the rink.

"See? You're a natural," Stephanie encouraged, her breath visible in the crisp air.

Jack laughed, the sound warm and rich. "I think that's more your influence than any latent talent on my part."

As they rounded a corner, Jack's skate caught an uneven patch of ice. He wobbled precariously, arms windmilling. Stephanie reacted instinctively, wrapping her arms around his waist to steady him. They came to a stop, pressed close together, both breathing a little harder than the gentle exercise warranted.

"My hero," Jack murmured, his face mere inches from hers.

Stephanie felt her cheeks flush, and not just from the cold. "Just looking out for my newest regular customer," she quipped, trying to lighten the suddenly charged moment.

They resumed skating, but Stephanie noticed Jack seemed more relaxed now, his movements becoming smoother with each lap. She found herself stealing glances at him, admiring the way the wind tousled his dark hair and the determined set of his jaw as he concentrated on his balance.

"You know," Jack said after a while, "I think I'm starting to see the appeal of small-town life. This beats dodging taxi cabs any day."

Stephanie's heart swelled with pride for her beloved Hollybrook. "Just wait until you see the rest of our Christmas traditions. We've only scratched the surface."

As they glided across the smooth ice, surrounded by the laughter of families and the soft glow of Christmas lights, Stephanie realized she couldn't remember the last time she'd felt so carefree and happy. She snuck another look at Jack, wondering if he felt it too - this undeniable magic in the air, full of possibility and the promise of something wonderful just beginning.

Stephanie gently tugged on Jack's arm. "Oh, you've got to see this!" she exclaimed, her breath forming little puffs in the crisp night air. "There's a street nearby that goes all out with decorations. It's like stepping into a Christmas card!"

Jack's lips curved into an intrigued smile. "Lead the way, Christmas cookie queen," he teased, falling into step beside her.

As they rounded the corner onto Maple Lane, Stephanie felt a familiar thrill course through her. The street before them was transformed into a winter wonderland, each house trying to outdo the next with dazzling light displays, inflatable Santas, and glittering reindeer.

"Wow," Jack breathed, his eyes wide with wonder. "I've never seen anything like this."

Stephanie beamed, drinking in his reaction. "It gets better every year. The neighbors have a friendly competition going."

They strolled down the sidewalk, their shoulders brushing. Stephanie pointed out her favorite displays, from the house with thousands of twinkling icicle lights to the one with a full nativity scene complete with live sheep.

"Look at that one!" Stephanie gasped, coming to a stop in front of a house that seemed to glow from within. Thousands of white lights outlined every eave and window, while rainbow-hued bulbs adorned perfectly trimmed hedges. In the center of the lawn stood a massive Christmas tree, its branches heavy with ornaments that glinted in the light.

"It's beautiful," Jack murmured, his voice soft with awe.

Stephanie nodded, feeling a lump form in her throat. "My grandmother and I used to walk this street every Christmas Eve," she said, her voice wistful. "She'd tell me stories about each ornament on our tree at home."

Jack turned to her, his expression gentle. "That sounds like a wonderful tradition."

"It was," Stephanie agreed, blinking back the hint of tears. "What about you? Any special holiday memories?"

Jack was quiet for a moment, his gaze fixed on the twinkling lights. "My dad and I would always make gingerbread houses," he said finally. "Well, I'd make them, and he'd eat half the candy before it made it onto the roof."

Stephanie laughed, the sound ringing out in the quiet night. "Sounds like my kind of architect!"

As they stood there, bathed in the warm glow of Christmas lights, Stephanie felt a sense of peace settle over her. She snuck a glance at Jack, noting the softness in his eyes as he took in the festive scene. In that moment, surrounded by the magic of the season, Stephanie realized that perhaps the best traditions were the ones yet to be made.

As they turned back towards the town square, a gust of chilly wind nipped at Stephanie's cheeks, sending a shiver down her spine. The festive lights twinkled merrily against the darkening sky, casting a warm glow over the cobblestone streets.

"Oh!" Stephanie exclaimed, her eyes lighting up as she spotted a quaint café nestled between two boutiques. Golden light spilled from its frosted windows, and the scent of cinnamon and chocolate wafted through the air. "Jack, would you like to stop for some hot cocoa? Mabel's makes the best in town."

Jack's face brightened. "That sounds perfect. I'm starting to lose feeling in my toes."

Stephanie laughed, the sound as warm and inviting as the café itself. "We can't have that. Come on, let's get you warmed up."

They hurried across the street, the bell above the door chiming merrily as they entered. The café was a cozy haven, with plush armchairs, twinkling fairy lights, and the soft strains of "White Christmas" playing in the background.

"Over here," Stephanie said, leading Jack to a secluded corner table near a crackling fireplace. As they settled into their seats, she couldn't help but notice how the firelight danced across Jack's features, highlighting the warmth in his eyes.

"Two hot cocoas, please," Stephanie called to Mabel, who gave her a knowing wink.

"So," Jack said, leaning forward slightly, "tell me more about your bakery. How did you get started?"

Stephanie's eyes lit up, her passion evident in her voice. "Oh, it all began with my grandmother's recipe book..."

As they sipped their rich, velvety cocoa, their conversation flowed effortlessly. Stephanie found herself captivated by Jack's stories of his architectural projects, while he listened intently to her tales of bakery mishaps and triumphs.

With each passing moment, Stephanie felt a warmth growing in her chest that had nothing to do with the cocoa. She couldn't help but think that maybe, just maybe, this Christmas would bring her more than just the usual holiday cheer.

Stephanie set down her empty mug, a contented sigh escaping her lips. The warmth of the cocoa still lingered, but she felt a sudden urge to experience more of the Christmas magic swirling around them.

"You know," she said, "there's one more stop we absolutely have to make. It's not a proper Hollybrook Christmas tour without seeing our town's pride and joy."

Jack's eyebrows raised in curiosity. "And what might that be?"

Stephanie grinned, already reaching for her coat. "Our Christmas tree, of course! It's truly a sight to behold."

As they stepped out into the crisp night air, Stephanie's heart skipped a beat when Jack's hand found hers. She led him down the cobblestone path, their breaths visible in small puffs.

"There it is," Stephanie whispered as they rounded the corner.

Before them stood a magnificent pine, easily forty feet tall, its branches laden with twinkling lights and shimmering ornaments. The star atop sparkled like a beacon in the night sky.

"Wow," Jack breathed, his eyes wide with wonder. "It's beautiful."

Stephanie nodded, drinking in the sight. "Every year, it takes my breath away."

They stood in silence for a moment, the tree's soft glow illuminating their faces. Stephanie felt a sense of peace wash over her, mingled with a growing warmth that had nothing to do with the seasonal decorations.

"You know," she said softly, "I've always thought there's something magical about standing under a Christmas tree. Like anything's possible."

Jack turned to her, his eyes reflecting the twinkling lights. "I'm starting to see what you mean."

As they turned away from the majestic Christmas tree, Stephanie felt a gentle tug on her hand. Jack's fingers were still intertwined with hers, sending a pleasant warmth through her entire body despite the chilly night air.

"I hate to say it," Jack said, his voice low and tinged with reluctance, "but I suppose we should head back to the bakery. It's getting late."

Stephanie nodded, her chestnut hair bobbing slightly. "You're right. But let's take the scenic route, shall we?"

They set off down a quieter street, their footsteps crunching softly on the light dusting of snow. The houses lining the road were adorned with twinkling lights and festive decorations, each one a miniature winter wonderland.

"You know," Stephanie said, breaking the comfortable silence, "I don't think I've enjoyed a tour of Hollybrook quite this much before."

Jack's lips curved into a smile. "Neither have I. Though I must admit, the company might have something to do with that."

Stephanie felt a blush creep up her cheeks, and she was grateful for the dim lighting. "I'm glad you came, Jack. Sometimes I get so caught up in the bakery that I forget to take a moment and appreciate all of this."

As they walked, Stephanie found herself stealing glances at Jack. The soft glow of the streetlights illuminated his strong profile, and she couldn't help but notice how his eyes seemed to sparkle with newfound joy.

"Stephanie," Jack said suddenly, stopping in his tracks. "I want to thank you for tonight. For showing me that there's more to life than fancy restaurants and critical reviews. This... this feels real."

Stephanie's heart swelled at his words. "That's what Hollybrook is all about. Real people, real connections."

As Sugar & Spice came into view, Stephanie felt a twinge of sadness that their evening was coming to an end. But as Jack squeezed her hand gently, she realized that this wasn't an ending at all. It was just the beginning of something wonderful.

Chapter 7

The scent of cinnamon and nutmeg hung in the air as Stephanie Fields frantically rifled through drawers in her cozy bakery kitchen. Her fingers trembled slightly as she pushed aside whisks and measuring cups, searching desperately for her grandmother's gingerbread recipe.

"Where is it?" she muttered, blowing a stray strand of chestnut hair out of her eyes. The warmth from the ovens wrapped around her like a blanket, but did little to soothe her rising panic.

Stephanie's gaze darted around the kitchen, taking in the cheerful red and green garlands draped along the walls. Any other day, the festive decorations would have filled her with joy. But right now, all she could think about was finding that recipe before the annual Christmas bake sale.

She yanked open another drawer, the metal clanging as utensils shifted. "Come on, come on," she whispered urgently.

The little bell above the bakery door chimed merrily, startling Stephanie. She whirled around to see Jack Carter stepping inside, a gust of crisp winter air following him.

"Whoa," he said, his blue eyes widening as he took in the chaos. "Looks like a flour bomb went off in here."

Stephanie glanced down at her flour-dusted apron and gave a sheepish laugh. "Oh, hey Jack. Just doing some last-minute prep for the bake sale."

Jack raised an eyebrow, his lips quirking into a half-smile. "Last-minute prep or kitchen demolition?"

"Very funny," Stephanie retorted, though she couldn't help returning his smile. There was something about Jack's calm presence that always managed to settle her nerves, even in moments of crisis like this.

He shrugged off his coat, revealing a cozy cable-knit sweater underneath. As he approached, Stephanie caught a whiff of pine and winter air clinging to him.

"What are you looking for?" Jack asked, his brow furrowing with concern as he watched Stephanie resume her frantic search.

She sighed, running a flour-covered hand through her messy bun. "My grandmother's gingerbread recipe. I can't find it anywhere and the bake sale is in two hours!"

Jack's eyes softened with understanding. "Mind if I lend a hand? Four eyes are better than two, right?"

Stephanie hesitated for a moment, torn between her independent nature and the genuine offer of help. Finally, she nodded gratefully. "That would be amazing, thank you."

As Jack rolled up his sleeves, ready to join the search, Stephanie couldn't help but feel a spark of warmth that had nothing to do with the ovens. Maybe, just maybe, this crisis wouldn't be so bad with Jack by her side.

Stephanie's eyes narrowed as she watched Jack reach for a stack of recipe cards. "I've already checked those," she snapped, snatching them away. "And I don't need your help. I can handle this myself."

The warmth in Jack's eyes dimmed slightly, but he didn't back down. "Stephanie, I'm just trying to—"

"To what?" she interrupted, her voice sharp with frustration. "Swoop in and save the day? I'm not some damsel in distress, Jack. I've been running this bakery just fine without you."

Stephanie turned her back on him, furiously rifling through a drawer filled with measuring cups and whisks. The metal utensils clanged together, mirroring the tension in the air. Her heart raced, panic rising with each passing second. Where was that recipe?

Jack's steady voice cut through her spiraling thoughts. "I know you can handle it, Stephanie. You're the most capable person I know." He paused, and she could feel his gaze on her back. "But sometimes it's okay to accept help, even if you don't need it."

Stephanie's shoulders slumped slightly, but she didn't turn around. "I appreciate the offer, Jack, but this is my grandmother's recipe. It's... personal."

"I understand," Jack said softly. The gentleness in his tone made Stephanie's chest tighten. "How about I just keep you company while you look? No helping, just moral support."

Despite herself, Stephanie felt a small smile tugging at her lips. She turned to face him, taking in his patient expression and the sincerity in those blue eyes. "Fine," she conceded. "But no touching anything. And if you start critiquing my organization system, you're out."

Jack held up his hands in mock surrender, a playful glint in his eye. "Wouldn't dream of it. Your chaotic filing method is clearly working wonders."

As Stephanie resumed her search, she couldn't help but feel a flicker of gratitude for Jack's presence. Maybe having him around wasn't so bad after all.

Stephanie exhaled sharply, her chestnut hair falling loose from its messy bun as she turned to face Jack. "Alright, fine. You can help. But follow my lead, okay?"

Jack nodded, a hint of a smile playing on his lips. "Of course. Where do we start?"

Stephanie's eyes darted around the bakery, her mind racing. "I've already checked the usual spots. Let's try the storage room."

As they made their way to the back, the warm scent of cinnamon and nutmeg enveloped them. Stephanie's fingers twitched nervously, longing to be kneading dough instead of rifling through papers.

"I'll take this side," Jack said, gesturing to a neat row of shelves.

Stephanie nodded distractedly, already diving into a cluttered corner. She yanked open drawers, scattering measuring spoons and cookie cutters. "It has to be here somewhere," she muttered, more to herself than to Jack.

Meanwhile, Jack methodically sifted through stacks of papers, his movements calm and deliberate. The contrast between their approaches was stark.

"Found anything?" Stephanie called out, her voice tight with frustration.

"Not yet," Jack replied evenly. "But we've only just started. Try to relax, Stephanie. We'll find it."

Stephanie huffed, reaching for a high shelf. "Easy for you to say. You're not the one whose entire Christmas baking schedule is about to be derailed by a missing rec-"

Her words cut off as her fingers caught the edge of a flour canister. It teetered precariously before tipping over, showering them both in a cloud of white.

"Oh no!" Stephanie gasped, coughing and waving her hand in front of her face.

Jack blinked, his dark hair now dusted with flour. "Well," he said, a smile tugging at his lips, "I suppose this is one way to get into the holiday spirit. We look like we've been caught in a snowstorm."

Despite her stress, Stephanie felt a giggle bubble up in her throat. "I'm so sorry, Jack. I didn't mean to-"

Her apology was interrupted as she stepped forward, slipping on the flour-covered floor. She stumbled, arms windmilling, and crashed into Jack. He caught her instinctively, but the momentum sent them both tumbling into a nearby shelf.

A cascade of parchment paper rolls rained down, unraveling as they fell. Within seconds, Stephanie found herself pressed against Jack's chest, both of them wrapped in layers of parchment like some sort of culinary mummy.

"Are you okay?" Jack asked, his voice a low rumble she could feel through his chest.

Stephanie looked up, meeting his concerned gaze. A laugh escaped her, starting small but quickly growing until she was shaking with mirth. "I'm fine," she managed between giggles. "But I think we might need to add 'gift wrapping' to your list of talents."

Jack's rich laughter joined hers, filling the small room with warmth. As their eyes met again, Stephanie felt something shift. Maybe letting Jack help wasn't such a disaster after all.

Stephanie's laughter faded as she realized how close she was to Jack, still entangled in parchment paper. She cleared her throat and took a step back, nearly tripping again.

"Careful there," Jack said, reaching out to steady her. "We wouldn't want you to fall and bruise that sharp wit of yours."

Stephanie rolled her eyes, but a smile played at the corners of her mouth. "Oh please, as if your clumsy attempts at helping haven't caused enough chaos already. I'm surprised you haven't managed to set fire to the place yet."

Jack raised an eyebrow, a glint of amusement in his blue eyes. "I'll have you know, I've been known to set many things ablaze – hearts, mostly. Though I suppose in your case, it might just be your temper."

Stephanie felt a flush creep up her neck, unsure if it was from annoyance or something else entirely. "Very funny, Mr. Food Critic. I'd like to see you try to bake a gingerbread house without that recipe."

As Jack opened his mouth to retort, his phone buzzed loudly in his pocket. He fished it out, brow furrowing as he read the screen.

"Everything okay?" Stephanie asked, curiosity overriding her irritation.

Jack hesitated, his earlier playfulness evaporating. "It's... an email. From my old editor in New York. They're offering me my job back – head food critic for the entire Eastern seaboard."

Stephanie felt her heart sink, though she wasn't entirely sure why. "Oh," she said softly. "That's... quite an opportunity."

Jack nodded, his eyes distant. "It is. I'd be lying if I said I hadn't missed the excitement sometimes. The high-profile restaurants, the cutting-edge cuisine..."

As he spoke, Stephanie couldn't help but picture Jack leaving Hollybrook, returning to the glittering world of New York's culinary scene. She was surprised by the pang of loss that accompanied the thought.

"But?" she prompted, sensing his hesitation.

Jack's gaze refocused on her, something unreadable in his expression. "But there's something to be said for small-town charm. For bakeries that smell like cinnamon and nutmeg, and bakers who aren't afraid to put a food critic in his place."

Stephanie felt her cheeks warm, unsure how to respond. Before she could, Jack's phone buzzed again, breaking the moment.

"You should probably answer that," she said, turning back to the mess of flour and parchment. "I'll just... keep looking for that recipe."

As she bent to clean up, Stephanie found herself wondering why the thought of Jack leaving suddenly felt so much worse than his initial arrival in Hollybrook had.

Stephanie sighed, brushing a stray lock of hair from her forehead, leaving a smudge of flour in its wake. She reached for another drawer, her fingers grazing the worn wood, when suddenly Jack's hand shot out, grabbing her wrist.

"Wait," he said, his blue eyes sparkling with excitement. "Look at this."

Stephanie's gaze followed his to a small scrap of paper peeking out from beneath a stack of baking pans. Her heart leapt. "Could it be?"

Together, they carefully lifted the heavy pans, revealing a familiar recipe card covered in her grandmother's looping handwriting.

"The gingerbread recipe!" Stephanie exclaimed, snatching it up. "But how did it end up here?"

Jack chuckled, a warm sound that filled the kitchen. "Sometimes the things we're looking for are hiding in plain sight."

Stephanie felt a smile tugging at her lips, the first genuine one she'd shared with Jack. "I guess we make a pretty good team after all."

With renewed energy, they set about organizing the bakery. The warm, spicy scent of cinnamon and cloves wafted through the air as Stephanie preheated the ovens. Jack methodically wiped down counters, the sleeves of his button-down rolled up to reveal strong forearms.

"So," Stephanie ventured, measuring out flour, "what made you trade New York's culinary scene for small-town Hollybrook anyway?"

Jack paused, considering. "I guess I was looking for something... real. Authentic. In New York, everything was about the next big trend, the flashiest presentation. But here?" He gestured around the cozy bakery. "Here, I can smell the love baked into every cookie."

Stephanie felt her cheeks flush, oddly pleased by his assessment. She opened her mouth to respond when the timer on the oven dinged, filling the bakery with its cheerful chime.

Stephanie turned to pull a tray of golden-brown sugar cookies from the oven, the scent of vanilla and buttery sweetness enveloping them both. As she set the tray on the cooling rack, she caught Jack's gaze lingering on her, a softness in his blue eyes she hadn't noticed before.

"You know," Stephanie said, her voice quieter than she intended, "I misjudged you, Jack. I thought you were just here to criticize, but... you've been genuinely helpful."

Jack's eyebrows rose slightly, surprise evident on his face. "I'm glad you can see that now," he replied, a hint of relief in his tone. "I never meant to come across as a threat, Stephanie. Your bakery, your passion – it's something special."

Stephanie felt a warmth spreading through her chest that had nothing to do with the heat from the ovens. She busied herself with arranging cookies on a festive platter, trying to sort through her conflicting emotions.

"I suppose I've been a bit... defensive," she admitted, stealing a glance at Jack. "It's just, this bakery means everything to me. The thought of losing it, or having someone swoop in and change it..."

Jack stepped closer, his presence both comforting and unsettling. "Stephanie, I understand. But you don't have to face everything alone. Sometimes, letting people in can lead to wonderful surprises."

Stephanie's heart fluttered traitorously. She found herself wanting to believe him, to trust in the warmth of his smile and the sincerity in his eyes. But a nagging fear held her back.

"It's not that simple," she murmured, more to herself than to Jack. "I've worked so hard to build this place, to keep my grandmother's legacy alive. The idea of risking it all..."

Jack's hand hesitated for a moment before gently touching her arm. "Who says you'd be risking anything? Stephanie, you've created something magical here. I'm not here to change that – I'm here because I want to be a part of it."

Stephanie looked up, meeting Jack's gaze. For a moment, the bakery faded away, and all she could see was the earnest hope in his eyes, mirroring her own vulnerable longing for connection.

The moment stretched, charged with unspoken possibilities. Stephanie's breath caught in her throat as she found herself leaning slightly towards Jack. The scent of cinnamon and vanilla enveloped them, a sweet reminder of their shared passion for baking.

Suddenly, Jack's phone buzzed loudly, shattering the moment. He fumbled to silence it, but not before Stephanie caught a glimpse of the caller ID: "NYC Executive Search."

"I... I should take this," Jack said, his voice strained. He stepped away, leaving Stephanie feeling oddly bereft.

As Jack spoke in hushed tones by the kitchen door, Stephanie busied herself reorganizing a shelf of sprinkles and edible glitter. Her mind raced. What was that call about? Was Jack planning to leave Hollybrook?

The thought sent an unexpected pang through her chest. She realized, with a jolt of surprise, that she'd grown accustomed to his presence, his quiet support, his infuriating ability to make her smile even when she was determined to be annoyed.

Jack returned, his expression unreadable. "Stephanie, I—"

A loud crash from the front of the bakery cut him off. They both rushed to investigate, finding a toppled display of gingerbread house kits scattered across the floor.

"Oh no," Stephanie groaned, kneeling to gather the fallen boxes. "These were supposed to be for tomorrow's workshop!"

As they worked to salvage what they could, Stephanie's fingers brushed against something wedged beneath the display stand. She pulled it out, her eyes widening in disbelief.

"My grandmother's recipe book!" she exclaimed, clutching the worn leather volume to her chest. "It must have fallen behind here when I was rearranging things last week."

She looked up at Jack, a mix of joy and embarrassment coloring her cheeks. "I can't believe it was here all along."

Jack smiled, but there was a hint of sadness in his eyes that made Stephanie's heart clench. "I'm glad you found it," he said softly. "Listen, Stephanie, about that call..."

Before he could continue, the bakery's bell chimed as a group of excited customers bustled in, their voices filling the air with cheerful chatter.

Stephanie hesitated, torn between her duty to her customers and her desperate need to hear what Jack had to say. The unfinished conversation hung between them, heavy with promise and uncertainty.

Stephanie's gaze darted between Jack and the incoming customers, her heart racing. She clutched the recipe book tighter, as if it could anchor her in this moment of indecision.

"I... I should probably..." she began, gesturing weakly towards the counter.

Jack nodded, holding a storm of emotions. "Of course. You go ahead. We can talk later."

As Stephanie turned to greet her customers, the scent of cinnamon and nutmeg wafted through the air, a bittersweet reminder of the Christmas spirit that usually filled her with joy. Now, it only intensified the knot in her stomach.

She plastered on a smile, her voice warm but slightly strained as she addressed the group. "Welcome to Sugar & Spice! What can I get for you today?"

While attending to the patrons, Stephanie couldn't help but steal glances at Jack. He lingered near the gingerbread display, straightening boxes with careful precision. His movements were measured, but she could see the tension in his shoulders.

"These gingerbread cookies smell divine!" an elderly woman exclaimed, drawing Stephanie's attention back to her task.

"Thank you," Stephanie replied, her cheeks flushing. "It's my grandmother's recipe, actually. The one I just found."

As she boxed up treats and rang up orders, her mind raced. What was Jack going to say about that call? Was he leaving Hollybrook? The thought sent a chill through her that had nothing to do with the winter weather outside.

When the last customer left, the bakery fell into an uneasy silence. Stephanie turned to face Jack, her heart pounding so loudly she was sure he could hear it.

"Jack, I—"

"Stephanie, about—"

They both spoke at once, then stopped, sharing a nervous laugh that did little to ease the tension.

"You go first," Stephanie said softly, bracing herself for what might come next.

Jack took a deep breath, his eyes meeting hers with an intensity that made her breath catch. "Stephanie, I need to tell you something important. It's about my future... and possibly ours."

The word 'ours' hung in the air between them, filled with both promise and uncertainty. Stephanie found herself frozen, equal parts hopeful and terrified of what Jack might say next. The clock on the wall ticked loudly, marking each passing second of this pivotal moment in their journey.

Chapter 8

The scent of cinnamon and vanilla hung thick in the air as Stephanie Fields rolled out another sheet of cookie dough. Her fingers worked quickly, dusted with flour, as she hummed along to "Jingle Bell Rock" playing softly in the background. She glanced over at Jack Carter, who was meticulously piping green and red icing onto a tray of sugar cookies nearby.

"Those look beautiful," Stephanie said warmly, admiring Jack's handiwork. His steady hands moved with practiced precision, creating delicate swirls and patterns.

Jack looked up, a rare smile tugging at his lips. "Thanks. I'm trying to channel my inner pastry artist."

Stephanie chuckled. "Well, you're doing a great job. I think these might be the prettiest cookies we've ever had at the Christmas Eve tasting."

She turned back to her dough, rolling it out to the perfect thickness. The wooden pin glided smoothly as she worked, her movements efficient after years of practice. The kitchen was cozy, filled with the warmth from the ovens and twinkling lights strung along the walls.

"I still can't believe you talked me into helping with all this," Jack said, his deep voice tinged with amusement. "I thought my days of cookie decorating were long behind me."

Stephanie grinned. "Oh come on, where's your Christmas spirit? Besides, I needed an extra set of hands and yours are perfect for the job."

She realized how that sounded and felt a blush creep up her cheeks. Thankfully, Jack seemed focused on his task and didn't notice her embarrassment.

Trying to distract herself, Stephanie grabbed a cookie cutter and began pressing out shapes. The metal edge sliced cleanly through the dough as Christmas trees and stars emerged.

"Can you pass me that spatula?" she asked, gesturing towards the utensil just out of reach.

"Sure, here you go—" Jack started to say.

As he turned, spatula in hand, Stephanie took a step back at the same moment. Her hip bumped against Jack's arm, knocking the tray he was holding. Time seemed to slow as she watched the beautifully decorated cookies slide off the tray and tumble towards the floor.

"Oh no!" Stephanie gasped, instinctively reaching out to try and catch them.

But it was too late. The cookies hit the ground with a resounding crash, shattering into pieces. Green and red icing splattered across the tile floor.

For a moment, they both stared at the mess in dismay. Stephanie's heart sank as she took in Jack's crestfallen expression. All that hard work, ruined in an instant because of her clumsiness.

"Jack, I'm so sorry," she said, her voice filled with regret. "I should have been more careful."

He let out a heavy sigh, running a hand through his dark hair. "It's alright. Accidents happen."

Stephanie could see the frustration in his eyes, despite his attempt at reassurance. She felt terrible, knowing how much time and effort he'd put into decorating those cookies.

"Let me clean this up," she said quickly, already moving to grab the broom and dustpan.

"I'll help," Jack insisted, kneeling down to start gathering the larger pieces.

As they worked side by side to clean up the mess, Stephanie couldn't help but feel a spark of warmth at Jack's willingness to pitch in. Maybe there was hope for his Christmas spirit after all.

Barking Up The Wrong Bakery

As Stephanie swept up the last of the crumbs, she let out a weary sigh. The sweet scent of vanilla and cinnamon that usually lifted her spirits now felt cloying, a reminder of the mounting pressure she faced.

"Everything alright?" Jack asked, his blue eyes studying her with concern.

Stephanie hesitated, then decided to confide in him. "It's just... this deadline from Peter Hamilton. And the town gossip about selling the bakery." She leaned on her broom, feeling the weight of it all. "Sometimes it feels like too much."

Jack's expression softened. "That's a lot to handle, especially during the holidays."

The warmth of his understanding wrapped around Stephanie like a cozy blanket. She continued, "I love this bakery. It's not just a business, it's..." She gestured around the quaint space, taking in the twinkling fairy lights and garlands adorning the walls. "It's the heart of Hollybrook's Christmas."

"I can see that," Jack nodded, his voice gentle. "You've created something special here, Stephanie."

His words bolstered her, but doubt still nagged. "But what if expanding is the right move? What if I'm holding the bakery back?"

Jack's brow furrowed thoughtfully. "Well, growth doesn't have to mean losing what makes this place unique. It could bring new opportunities, maybe even allow you to spread that Christmas magic further."

Stephanie felt a flicker of indignation. "But at what cost? Our personal touch, the connections we've built with every customer?" She could feel her cheeks growing warm as she spoke more passionately. "This isn't just about profit margins, Jack. It's about community."

"I understand that," Jack countered, his own voice rising slightly. "But think about how many more people you could reach, how many more lives you could brighten with your baking."

As they debated, the aroma of freshly baked gingerbread wafted through the air, a poignant reminder of everything at stake. Stephanie's heart raced, torn between tradition and the potential for something new.

Stephanie's eyes flashed, her voice trembling with emotion. "You don't understand, Jack. This bakery isn't just a business to me. It's my grandmother's legacy, it's... it's everything I am." She gripped the edge of the flour-dusted counter, knuckles white.

Jack ran a hand through his dark hair, frustration evident in his tense shoulders. "Stephanie, sometimes change is necessary for survival. You're so resistant to even considering the possibilities—"

"And you're so caught up in the bottom line that you can't see the heart of what makes this place special!" Stephanie cut him off, the words tumbling out before she could stop them.

The air between them crackled with tension, the cheerful tinkling of Christmas music from the speakers a stark contrast to their heated exchange. Stephanie opened her mouth to say more, but the jingling of the bell above the door stopped her short.

In an instant, both Stephanie and Jack's demeanors transformed. Stephanie plastered on a warm smile, brushing flour from her festive red apron. "Welcome to Sugar & Spice!" she called out cheerfully, her voice betraying none of the turmoil from moments before.

Jack smoothly stepped beside her, his own smile polite and professional. "How can we help you today?" he asked, effortlessly slipping into a united front with Stephanie.

As they greeted the customer, Stephanie's mind raced. How had their conversation escalated so quickly? And why did Jack's opinion matter so much to her? She pushed the thoughts aside, focusing on the warm, spicy scent of cinnamon and the task at hand. There would be time to sort through her feelings later. For now, there were cookies to bake and Christmas cheer to spread.

Stephanie watched as the customer, an elderly woman with snow-white hair and twinkling eyes, approached the display case. The scent of freshly baked gingerbread mingled with the pine aroma from the wreath on the door, creating a truly festive atmosphere.

"I'm looking for something special for my grandchildren," the woman said, her gaze roaming over the colorful array of Christmas cookies.

"Of course," Stephanie replied warmly. "Jack, why don't you tell her about our holiday sampler?" She glanced at him, their eyes meeting briefly.

Jack nodded, smoothly taking the lead. "Our holiday sampler is perfect for families," he explained, gesturing to a beautifully packaged assortment. "It includes Stephanie's famous sugar cookies, which are a town favorite."

Barking Up The Wrong Bakery

Stephanie felt a flutter in her chest at his praise. Despite their disagreement, Jack's support of her baking skills was unwavering. She chimed in, "And we've added some new flavors this year, like cranberry orange and chocolate peppermint."

As they worked together to help the customer, Stephanie couldn't help but marvel at how seamlessly they complemented each other. Jack's culinary knowledge perfectly balanced her homey charm.

"You two make quite the team," the elderly woman remarked with a knowing smile as she left with her purchase.

The bell jingled again, leaving Stephanie and Jack alone in the sudden silence. The tension from earlier crept back, hanging heavy in the air like the aroma of spiced cider.

Stephanie sighed, running a flour-dusted hand through her hair. "Jack, I... I think we need to talk about what happened earlier."

Jack's blue eyes met hers, his expression softening. "You're right. This isn't like us, Stephanie. We're usually so in sync."

"I know," Stephanie replied, her voice barely above a whisper. "Maybe we've both been under too much pressure with the upcoming event. But we can't let it affect our work or... our friendship."

Jack nodded, a small smile tugging at his lips. "Agreed. How about we take a breather and then tackle these cookie orders together? Just like old times?"

Stephanie felt the tension in her shoulders ease. "That sounds perfect. And Jack? I'm sorry for what I said earlier. I know you care about this place too."

As they moved back to their work stations, Stephanie felt a renewed sense of purpose. They might not agree on everything, but their shared love for baking and bringing joy to others was stronger than any disagreement. The sweet scent of vanilla and the warmth of the ovens enveloped them, a reminder of why they both loved this bakery so much.

Stephanie brushed the remaining flour off her hands and untied her apron. "You know what? I think we both could use a breath of fresh air. Care to join me for a quick walk around town?"

Jack's eyebrows rose in surprise, but a smile quickly replaced his shocked expression. "That sounds like just what we need. Let me grab my coat."

As they stepped out of Sugar & Spice, the crisp winter air nipped at their cheeks. Stephanie inhaled deeply, the scent of pine and woodsmoke filling her lungs. The tension that had been building inside the bakery seemed to dissipate with each step they took on the snow-dusted sidewalk.

"Oh, look!" Stephanie exclaimed, pointing at the town square. "They've finished putting up the Christmas tree."

Jack followed her gaze, his blue eyes reflecting the twinkling lights. "It's beautiful. Reminds me of the tree we used to have in Central Park."

Stephanie glanced at him curiously. "I bet Christmas in New York was quite a spectacle."

"It was," Jack nodded, his voice tinged with nostalgia. "But there's something special about small-town celebrations. It feels more... intimate."

As they strolled past storefronts adorned with garlands and ribbons, Stephanie found herself relaxing. The soft glow of Christmas lights cast a warm ambiance over the street, and the sound of distant carolers filled the air.

"You know," Stephanie began, her breath visible in the cold air, "my favorite holiday memory is baking cookies with my grandmother. The whole house would smell like cinnamon and butter."

Jack chuckled softly. "That sounds lovely. For me, it was helping my dad string lights on the house. We'd always end up tangled in them somehow."

Stephanie laughed, picturing a young Jack wrapped in a mess of Christmas lights. "I can just imagine! Did you ever get them untangled?"

As they continued their walk, sharing stories and laughter, Stephanie felt a warmth spreading through her chest that had nothing to do with her cozy sweater. She realized that despite their differences, she and Jack shared a deep appreciation for the magic of the holiday season.

The aroma of roasted chestnuts and mulled wine suddenly wafted through the air, causing Stephanie to pause mid-step. Her eyes widened as she spotted the source: a quaint Christmas market tucked away in the town square.

"Oh, Jack! Look!" she exclaimed, her face lighting up with childlike wonder. "I completely forgot the market was happening tonight. Let's check it out!"

Jack's lips curved into a soft smile as he observed Stephanie's excitement. "Lead the way," he said, gesturing forward with a sweep of his arm.

They meandered through the market, their shoulders occasionally brushing as they navigated the cheerful crowd. Stephanie's eyes danced from stall to stall, taking in the handcrafted ornaments, artisanal chocolates, and festive knick-knacks.

"Try this," Jack said, offering her a small paper cup. "It's spiced apple cider. Best I've ever tasted."

Stephanie took a sip, the warm liquid spreading a comforting heat through her body. "Mmm, that's delicious! But I think I could give it a run for its money with my secret recipe," she teased, a playful glint in her eye.

As they sampled more treats, a street performer dressed as an elf began juggling candy canes nearby. Stephanie burst into laughter as the elf "accidentally" dropped one, only to catch it with his foot and flip it back into the rotation.

"Now that's talent," Jack chuckled, his blue eyes crinkling at the corners.

They found themselves gravitating towards a cozy hot cocoa stand, festooned with twinkling fairy lights. Jack insisted on treating Stephanie, and soon they were cradling steaming mugs topped with generous swirls of whipped cream.

"You know," Stephanie began, her voice softening, "I sometimes forget how magical Hollybrook can be. Especially during the holidays."

Jack nodded, his gaze sweeping over the festive scene. "It's special, that's for sure. I can see why you're so passionate about preserving its charm."

Stephanie felt a pang in her chest, remembering their earlier disagreement. "And I can understand why you see the potential for growth," she admitted. "I suppose we both just want what's best for the town."

"And for your bakery," Jack added gently. "I hope you know that, despite our differences, I truly believe in what you've built, Stephanie."

Their eyes met over their cocoa mugs, and Stephanie felt a flutter in her stomach that had nothing to do with the sweet treat. In that moment, surrounded by the warmth and joy of the Christmas market, she realized that their shared love for Hollybrook ran deeper than any business decision.

"Thank you, Jack," she said softly, a genuine smile spreading across her face. "I'm glad we took this walk. Sometimes it's easy to lose sight of what really matters, especially during the busy holiday season."

Jack's expression mirrored her own, his earlier reserve melting away. "Me too, Stephanie. Me too."

The bell above the bakery door jingled merrily as Stephanie and Jack stepped inside, the warmth enveloping them like a cozy blanket. The rich aroma of vanilla and cinnamon wafted through the air, a stark contrast to the crisp winter breeze they'd left behind.

Stephanie inhaled deeply, letting the familiar scents wash over her. "Nothing quite like coming back to the bakery," she said, her eyes sparkling. "It always feels like coming home."

Jack nodded, a small smile playing at the corners of his mouth. "I can see why. It's impossibly inviting in here."

As they shed their coats, Stephanie felt a sense of purpose coursing through her veins. The tension that had clouded the air earlier had dissipated, replaced by an easy camaraderie.

"Ready to tackle these Christmas cookies?" she asked, tying her apron with practiced ease.

"Absolutely," Jack replied, rolling up his sleeves. "Where do you want me?"

They fell into a rhythm, moving around each other with a newfound synchronicity. Stephanie rolled out dough while Jack prepped the royal icing, their movements fluid and purposeful.

"You know," Stephanie mused, carefully cutting out star-shaped cookies, "I think we make a pretty good team."

Jack glanced up from his work, "I'd have to agree. Who knew a former food critic and a small-town baker could work so well together?"

Stephanie laughed, the sound light and genuine. "Stranger things have happened, I suppose. Especially in Hollybrook during Christmas."

As they worked, their conversation flowed effortlessly, punctuated by the gentle hum of the mixer and the occasional clink of baking sheets. Stephanie found herself marveling at how easy it felt, how natural. It was as if their earlier disagreement had cleared the air, allowing them to see each other more clearly.

"Jack," she said softly, pausing in her work, "I'm glad you're here. Really. I don't think I could pull off this Cookie Tasting event without you."

Jack's expression softened, and he reached out to gently squeeze her flour-dusted hand. "There's nowhere else I'd rather be, Stephanie. Now, let's make these the best Christmas cookies Hollybrook has ever tasted."

Stephanie's heart warmed at Jack's touch, and she found herself smiling as they continued their work. The bakery was filled with the comforting aroma of vanilla and cinnamon, mingling with the crisp scent of freshly baked cookies.

As the last batch came out of the oven, Stephanie sighed contentedly. "I think we've done it, Jack. These look amazing."

Jack nodded, his eyes roaming over the array of festive cookies. "They do. But more importantly, how do you feel about everything now?"

Stephanie paused, considering his question. She wiped her hands on her apron and leaned against the counter, her brown eyes meeting Jack's blue ones.

"Honestly? I feel... lighter. Like a weight has been lifted," she admitted. "I've been so caught up in the pressure of the franchise offer and what everyone else thinks, I almost forgot why I started this bakery in the first place."

Jack moved closer, his voice soft. "And why did you?"

"To bring joy to people through food," Stephanie replied, her voice filled with emotion. "To create a place where the community could come together and feel at home."

Jack nodded, a gentle smile playing on his lips. "That's what makes Sugar & Spice special, Stephanie. It's not just about the cookies or the business decisions. It's about the heart you put into everything you do."

Stephanie felt a lump forming in her throat. "You really understand, don't you?"

"I do," Jack said, reaching out to tuck a stray strand of hair behind her ear. "And I want you to know, whatever you decide about the franchise offer, I'm here for you. Our friendship, this connection we have... it's more important than any business decision."

Stephanie's eyes glistened with unshed tears. "Thank you, Jack. That means more to me than you know."

In that quiet moment, surrounded by the fruits of their labor and the warmth of the bakery, Stephanie and Jack shared a look of understanding. Whatever challenges lay ahead, they would face them together, their bond stronger than any obstacle that might come their way.

Chapter 9

The soft glow of candlelight flickered across Stephanie's face as she sat across from Jack at a small table tucked in the corner of Sugar & Spice Bakery. The warmth from the nearby oven enveloped them like a cozy blanket, carrying the comforting scent of cinnamon and vanilla. Stephanie's fingers nervously traced the rim of her mug, the ceramic still warm from the peppermint hot chocolate she'd prepared earlier.

Jack took a deep breath, his broad shoulders rising and falling as he seemed to gather his thoughts. Stephanie found herself holding her own breath, captivated by the play of shadows across his chiseled features.

"I haven't always been the small-town guy you see before you," Jack began, his deep voice barely above a whisper. "Back in New York, I was... different. A food critic, actually."

Stephanie's eyebrows rose in surprise, but she remained silent, not wanting to interrupt his flow.

"It was a whirlwind of exclusive restaurants, champagne brunches, and cutthroat competition," he continued, a hint of weariness creeping into his tone. "Every meal was an opportunity to make or break someone's career with just a few words."

As Jack spoke, Stephanie couldn't help but picture him in a sleek suit, scribbling notes in a leather-bound journal while sampling exquisite dishes. It was so far removed from the man before her now, dressed in a soft flannel shirt with flour dusting his sleeve from where he'd brushed against her earlier.

"But the constant pressure, the endless stream of elaborate dishes... it all started to lose its flavor, you know?" Jack's piercing blue eyes met hers, seeking understanding.

Stephanie nodded, her heart aching for the emptiness she saw reflected in his gaze. She wanted to reach out, to offer comfort, but something held her back. Instead, she simply said, "That must have been incredibly draining."

Jack's lips quirked in a small, grateful smile. "It was. I found myself craving something simpler, more... authentic."

As he spoke, Stephanie's mind drifted to her own journey. The long nights perfecting recipes, the joy of seeing a customer's face light up at first bite of her creations. She understood the power of food to connect people, to bring joy in its purest form.

"Is that what brought you to Hollybrook?" she asked softly, genuinely curious about his path.

Jack nodded, his gaze drifting to the twinkling Christmas lights adorning the bakery's windows. "I needed a change. Somewhere I could rediscover the joy in food, in life." His eyes found hers again, a warmth kindling in their depths. "I never expected to find all of this."

Stephanie felt a blush creeping up her neck, wondering if the 'this' he referred to included her. She opened her mouth to respond, but the timer on the oven chimed, breaking the moment.

"Oh! The gingerbread!" she exclaimed, jumping to her feet. As she hurried to rescue her cookies, Stephanie's mind whirled with this new understanding of Jack. There was so much more to him than she'd realized, and she found herself eager to uncover every layer.

Stephanie's eyes widened as Jack's words sank in, her heart fluttering with a mix of surprise and empathy. The warm glow of the candlelight softened his features, revealing a vulnerability she'd never seen before. She leaned in, captivated by his story, the rich aroma of cinnamon and nutmeg from a nearby tray of freshly baked cookies enveloping them both.

"I had no idea," she breathed, her voice barely above a whisper. "It must have been such a difficult decision to leave everything behind."

Jack's blue eyes met hers, a hint of relief flickering across his face. "It was," he admitted, his fingers absently tracing the rim of his mug. "But coming here, to Hollybrook... it's been like rediscovering a part of myself I'd forgotten existed."

Stephanie felt a surge of warmth in her chest, touched by his honesty. She watched as Jack's gaze swept across the bakery, taking in the cheerful holiday decorations and the cozy nooks where regulars gathered.

"Your bakery, Stephanie," he said, his voice filled with genuine admiration, "it's more than just a place to get a great cookie. It's... it's the heart of this town."

Stephanie felt her cheeks flush at the compliment, a pleased smile tugging at her lips.

Jack continued, his voice growing softer. "I came to Hollybrook looking for a place where I could belong, where I could appreciate the simple joys again." He paused, a shy smile playing on his lips. "I never expected to find all of this... or someone like you."

Stephanie's heart skipped a beat, the unspoken connection between them hanging in the air like the delicate sugar snowflakes adorning her window display.

Stephanie's face softened, her warm brown eyes brimming with understanding and compassion. Without hesitation, she reached across the table, gently placing her hand over Jack's. The touch sent a small shiver through her, like the first spark of a Christmas light coming to life.

"Jack," she said softly, her voice as warm as freshly baked gingerbread, "I think I understand more than you know."

The scent of cinnamon and vanilla hung in the air as Stephanie took a deep breath, the familiar aromas giving her courage. "When I first opened Sugar & Spice, it wasn't just about selling pastries. It was about creating a home away from home."

She glanced around the bakery, taking in the twinkling fairy lights and the laughter of customers sharing hot cocoa and conversation. "Every cookie, every pie... they're more than just desserts. They're little pieces of joy I get to share with everyone who walks through that door."

Jack listened intently, his piercing blue eyes fixed on Stephanie's face. She could feel the warmth of his hand beneath hers, steady and comforting.

"This place," Stephanie continued, her voice thick with emotion, "it's become a symbol of love, of connection. On days when I'm up to my elbows in flour at 4 AM, it's knowing that I'm part of something bigger that keeps me going." She let out a small laugh. "Well, that and a lot of coffee."

Jack chuckled softly, the sound warming Stephanie more than any cup of hot chocolate ever could.

"I guess what I'm trying to say," Stephanie finished, giving Jack's hand a gentle squeeze, "is that I found my purpose in baking, in creating this little haven. And I'm so glad it's become a place where you can find what you're looking for too."

As Stephanie's words hung in the air, Jack's eyes lit up with a newfound appreciation. The soft glow of the bakery's warm lighting seemed to reflect in his gaze, mirroring the tenderness in Stephanie's own expression.

"Stephanie," Jack said, his voice low and filled with wonder, "what you've created here... it's extraordinary."

He glanced around the bakery, taking in the cozy nooks, the festive garlands, and the inviting aroma of cinnamon and vanilla that permeated the air. "I've been to some of the most acclaimed restaurants in New York, but none of them had this... this heart."

Stephanie felt a blush creep up her cheeks. "It's just a small-town bakery," she demurred.

"No," Jack insisted, leaning forward. "It's so much more than that. You've managed to bake love and community into every corner of this place. I can taste it in every bite, feel it in the laughter of your customers."

Their eyes met, and Stephanie's breath caught in her throat. Jack's usually guarded expression had softened, revealing a vulnerability that made her heart skip a beat.

"I never thought I'd find a place that felt like... home," Jack admitted, his fingers absently tracing patterns on the tablecloth. "But being here, in Hollybrook, in Sugar & Spice... it's like I've finally found where I belong."

Stephanie's lips curved into a warm smile, her eyes crinkling at the corners. "I'm so glad you found your way here, Jack," she said softly.

As they gazed at each other, Stephanie felt a surge of connection, a deepening of their bond that went beyond words. In that moment, she realized how much they had in common – two souls who had found their purpose in the warmth of a small town and the simple joy of sharing food with others.

Jack's smile widened, matching her own. "So am I, Stephanie," he replied, his voice barely above a whisper. "So am I."

Stephanie's heart swelled with gratitude, her eyes glistening in the soft candlelight. She reached across the table, gently placing her hand atop Jack's. The warmth of his skin sent a tingle up her arm.

"Jack," she began, her voice thick with emotion, "I can't tell you how much it means to me that you've shared this with me. Your honesty, your vulnerability..." She paused, swallowing the lump in her throat. "I'm truly honored to have you as part of Sugar & Spice, and..." she hesitated, then added softly, "part of my life."

The scent of cinnamon and vanilla lingered in the air, mingling with the rich aroma of freshly brewed coffee. Outside, a gentle snow had begun to fall, dusting the windowsills with a layer of crystalline white.

Jack's blue eyes locked onto Stephanie's, a mix of surprise and warmth dancing in their depths. He turned his hand over, giving her fingers a gentle squeeze. "Stephanie, I—" he started, then paused, collecting his thoughts. "This bakery, this town... you... it's all become so important to me." He took a deep breath, his shoulders squaring with determination. "I want you to know that I'm committed to supporting you and Sugar & Spice in every way I can."

Stephanie's eyebrows raised slightly, a questioning look crossing her face.

Jack leaned in, his voice low and earnest. "The upcoming Cookie Tasting event? I promise I'll do everything in my power to make it a success. Whatever you need – taste-testing, promotion, even washing dishes – I'm here for you."

A warm, appreciative chuckle escaped Stephanie's lips. "Even dishes? Now that's dedication!"

Stephanie's warm brown eyes shimmered with newfound determination, the soft candlelight reflecting in them like tiny stars. She leaned forward, her voice filled with a quiet intensity that made Jack's heart skip a beat.

"You know what, Jack? We're going to face whatever challenges come our way together," she declared, her words carrying the weight of a solemn promise. "Our love for Hollybrook, for Sugar & Spice - it's not just about baking anymore. It's about community, about bringing joy to people's lives."

Jack nodded, a small smile tugging at the corners of his mouth. "You're right," he agreed, his deep voice barely above a whisper. "It's about creating something meaningful, something that lasts."

Stephanie's gaze softened, her eyes never leaving Jack's. "Exactly. And together, we have the strength to overcome any obstacle that comes our way."

Without breaking eye contact, Stephanie reached across the table, her flour-dusted fingers seeking Jack's. As their hands met, Jack's larger ones enveloped hers, their fingers intertwining naturally, as if they'd been meant to fit together all along.

The touch sent a warm tingle up Stephanie's arm, and she marveled at how right it felt. In that moment, surrounded by the comforting scents of her bakery and the gentle glow of candlelight, Stephanie felt a sense of unity and shared purpose unlike anything she'd experienced before.

Jack's thumb traced small circles on the back of her hand, his touch as light as a snowflake. "Together," he echoed, the single word filled with promise.

The bakery settled into a comfortable silence, broken only by the soft crackle of candles and the distant hum of the refrigerator. Stephanie basked in the warmth of Jack's presence, feeling a profound sense of connection. The weight of running Sugar & Spice suddenly felt lighter, shared between them.

Jack's eyes crinkled at the corners as he gazed at her, a soft smile playing on his lips. Stephanie's heart fluttered, and she found herself thinking how his smile reminded her of the way fresh snow glistened in the morning sunlight.

After a moment, Stephanie reluctantly pulled her hand away, the loss of contact sending a small shiver through her. She glanced at the clock on
the wall, its gingerbread-shaped hands reminding her of their responsibilities.

"We should probably get back to work," Stephanie said, her voice tinged with both regret and renewed determination. "The Cookie Tasting event won't plan itself."

Barking Up The Wrong Bakery

Jack nodded, his eyes sparkling with enthusiasm. "You're right. And after our talk, I'm more excited than ever to make it a success."

Stephanie stood, smoothing down her flour-dusted apron. "Me too. I have a feeling this is going to be the best event Sugar & Spice has ever seen."

As they moved towards the kitchen, Stephanie couldn't help but feel a surge of joy. With Jack by her side, she knew they could face anything – even a bakery full of Christmas cookies waiting to be baked.

Stephanie and Jack rose from the table in tandem, their movements synchronized as if choreographed. The soft glow of the bakery's twinkling lights cast a warm halo around them, highlighting the flour dusting Jack's broad shoulders and the determined set of Stephanie's jaw.

"Ready to conquer some cookie dough?" Stephanie asked, her eyes sparkling with a mix of mischief and affection.

Jack chuckled, the sound rich and warm like freshly baked gingerbread. "Lead the way, Cookie Queen."

As they made their way to the kitchen, Stephanie's fingers brushed against Jack's, sending a jolt of electricity through her. She wondered if he felt it too, this invisible thread connecting them.

The aroma of cinnamon and vanilla enveloped them as they entered the kitchen. Stephanie's mind raced with possibilities for the Cookie Tasting event, her excitement bubbling over.

"I was thinking," she began, reaching for her favorite whisk, "what if we create a signature Hollybrook cookie for the event? Something that captures the spirit of our town?"

Jack's eyebrows raised in interest. "That's brilliant, Stephanie. What did you have in mind?"

As Stephanie explained her idea, her hands moved animatedly, nearly knocking over a jar of sprinkles. Jack caught it with lightning-fast reflexes, steadying it on the counter. Their eyes met, and Stephanie felt a warmth spread through her chest that had nothing to do with the heat of the ovens.

She couldn't help but think how natural it felt, working side by side with Jack in her kitchen. It was as if he had always been there, a missing piece she hadn't known was absent until now.

Chapter 10

The bakery plunged into darkness as the power cut out with a decisive click. Stephanie gasped, her hands freezing mid-roll on the gingerbread dough she'd been shaping.

"Jack?" she called out, blinking as her eyes adjusted to the sudden gloom. The rich scent of cinnamon and nutmeg still hung in the air, a stark contrast to the eerie silence that had fallen over Sugar & Spice.

"I'm here," Jack's calm voice came from somewhere near the front counter. "Don't move, I'll find a light."

Stephanie heard the shuffle of his footsteps and the soft thud of his hand meeting a wall. She couldn't help but smile despite the situation. Even in a crisis, Jack maintained his composure.

"There should be some flashlights in the supply closet," Stephanie said, carefully setting down her rolling pin. "And I think I have some candles in my office."

"On it," Jack replied. Stephanie heard him fumbling with the closet door, followed by the satisfying click of a flashlight switching on. A beam of light cut through the darkness, illuminating Jack's determined face.

"Oh, thank goodness," Stephanie sighed in relief. She wiped her flour-dusted hands on her apron and moved towards Jack, nearly tripping over a mixing bowl in her haste. "What on earth happened?"

Jack shrugged, his blue eyes reflecting the flashlight's glow. "Could be the storm. I heard the wind picking up earlier."

Barking Up The Wrong Bakery

Stephanie's heart sank as reality set in. "The Christmas Eve Cookie Tasting," she murmured, her voice barely above a whisper. "Jack, it's tomorrow night. How are we going to pull this off without power?"

She could feel panic rising in her chest, threatening to overwhelm her. The cookie tasting was the highlight of Hollybrook's holiday season, a tradition she'd inherited from her grandmother. The thought of disappointing the entire town made her stomach churn.

Jack must have sensed her distress because he placed a comforting hand on her shoulder. "Hey, we'll figure this out," he said softly. "Let's start by getting some more light in here, okay?"

Stephanie nodded, taking a deep breath to steady herself. "You're right. We need to stay calm and think this through."

As they worked together to light candles and set up battery-powered lanterns, Stephanie's mind raced with potential solutions. The warm glow of the candles cast dancing shadows on the walls, creating an oddly cozy atmosphere despite the circumstances.

"Okay," Stephanie said, her determination returning as she surveyed the softly lit bakery. "We have about 24 hours to save this event. We can do this, right?"

Jack's lips quirked into a small smile. "If anyone can pull off a Christmas miracle, it's you, Stephanie."

His words sent a flutter through her chest, momentarily distracting her from their predicament. She pushed the feeling aside, focusing on the task at hand.

"First things first," Stephanie declared, tying her chestnut hair into a tighter bun. "We need to salvage what we can from the refrigerators before everything spoils. Then we'll tackle the power issue."

As they worked side by side in the candlelit bakery, Stephanie couldn't help but feel a spark of hope. With Jack by her side and the spirit of Christmas in her heart, she was determined to make this cookie tasting the best one yet – power outage or not.

Stephanie's phone chimed, breaking the quiet rhythm of their work. She wiped her flour-dusted hands on her apron and reached for it, her brow furrowing as she read the message.

"Oh no," she groaned, her shoulders slumping. "The Mayor and the Chamber of Commerce president just canceled. They were our keynote speakers for the event."

Jack set down the tray of cookie dough he'd been organizing. "That's a significant blow. Did they give a reason?"

Stephanie shook her head, her warm brown eyes filled with disappointment. "Just a vague excuse about a last-minute conflict. This is a disaster, Jack. Without them, we'll lose a lot of publicity and credibility."

The scent of vanilla and cinnamon hung in the air, a bittersweet reminder of their predicament. Jack ran a hand through his dark hair, his blue eyes thoughtful. "We need to brainstorm alternatives. Who else in town has enough influence to draw a crowd?"

Stephanie paced the length of the bakery, the soft glow of candles illuminating her determined expression. "What about Mrs. Hemingway? She's been the town's unofficial historian for decades. People love her stories about Hollybrook's Christmas traditions."

Jack nodded, a smile tugging at his lips. "That's a great idea. And what if we reached out to Chef Marco from the Italian restaurant down the street? He's got quite a following."

"Oh! That's brilliant, Jack!" Stephanie exclaimed, her eyes lighting up. "We could turn it into a multicultural Christmas cookie event. Expand our horizons a bit."

As they bounced ideas back and forth, the initial disappointment began to fade, replaced by a growing excitement. Stephanie could feel the warmth of possibility spreading through her chest, mingling with the cozy aroma of freshly baked cookies.

"You know," Jack mused, his voice soft in the candlelit bakery, "this setback might actually lead to something even better than we originally planned."

Stephanie nodded, a smile spreading across her face. "You're right. It's not what we expected, but it could be exactly what Hollybrook needs this Christmas."

With renewed energy, they dove back into their preparations, the power outage momentarily forgotten as they worked together to bring their new vision to life.

The warmth of their collaboration quickly cooled as Stephanie and Jack found themselves at odds over the next steps. The flickering candlelight cast dancing shadows across their faces, highlighting the tension that had settled between them.

"Jack, we need to call everyone right now," Stephanie insisted, her voice tight with stress. "If we don't secure these replacements immediately, we'll lose our chance."

Jack shook his head. "Stephanie, it's past nine. We can't call people this late. It's unprofessional and might put them off entirely."

Stephanie's frustration bubbled over. "Unprofessional? This whole situation is unprofessional! We're working by candlelight, for heaven's sake!"

"I understand you're stressed, but—"

"No, you don't understand," Stephanie cut him off, her voice rising. "This isn't just about the event. It's about the people of Hollybrook. They're counting on us, on me, to make this Christmas special."

Jack's jaw tightened. "And staying up all night making frantic phone calls is going to accomplish that?"

Stephanie felt tears pricking at her eyes. She turned away, busying herself with reorganizing a tray of gingerbread men. The spicy scent of cinnamon and cloves usually comforted her, but now it only reminded her of all that was at stake.

"You don't get it, Jack," she said softly, her voice barely above a whisper. "This bakery, these events... they're not just my job. They're my life. My connection to this town, to my grandmother's legacy. If I fail..."

She trailed off, unable to voice her deepest fear. The weight of responsibility pressed down on her shoulders, as heavy as the darkness surrounding them.

Jack's expression softened. He stepped closer, the scent of his cologne mingling with the bakery's sweet aromas. "Stephanie, you're not going to fail. But you can't do everything alone, and you can't do it all tonight."

Stephanie turned to face him, her brown eyes shimmering with unshed tears. "Then what do we do? How do we save this?"

The silence stretched between them, filled only by the soft crackle of candle wicks and the distant sound of carolers on the street outside.

Stephanie took a deep breath, squaring her shoulders. "Okay, we need to focus on the power first. Everything else is moot if we can't even turn on the ovens."

Jack nodded, his blue eyes glinting with determination in the candlelight. "Agreed. Let's check the fuse box."

They moved in unison, Stephanie grabbing a flashlight from behind the counter while Jack carefully navigated around scattered baking supplies. The beam of light danced across the walls as they made their way to the back of the bakery.

"It's just past the storage room," Stephanie said, her voice echoing slightly in the darkened hallway. The familiar scents of vanilla and almond extract wafted from the shelves, a comforting reminder of normalcy amidst the chaos.

Jack reached the fuse box first, his tall frame casting a long shadow as Stephanie held the light steady. "Alright, let's see what we're dealing with," he muttered, opening the metal door with a creak.

Stephanie peered over his shoulder, her breath warm against his neck. "Anything obvious?"

"Not yet," Jack replied, his fingers tracing the labels on each switch. "Wait a second..." He paused, tapping one particular fuse. "This one's tripped. Probably overloaded from all the extra appliances we plugged in for the event prep."

Stephanie's heart leapt. "Can you fix it?"

Jack's lips curved into a small smile. "I think so. Here goes nothing."

With a firm click, he reset the switch. For a moment, nothing happened. Then, suddenly, the bakery hummed to life. Lights flickered on, the refrigerator motors whirred, and the gentle beep of the ovens warming up filled the air.

"Oh my god, Jack!" Stephanie exclaimed, barely resisting the urge to hug him. "You did it!"

Jack turned to face her, his usually reserved expression replaced by a genuine grin. "We did it, Stephanie. Teamwork, remember?"

Stephanie laughed, the sound bright and filled with relief. "I don't know about you, but I feel like I just won the lottery."

"Better than the lottery," Jack quipped. "We won electricity. Now, shall we get back to those cookies?"

As they walked back to the main area, Stephanie felt a renewed sense of hope. The warm glow of the bakery lights seemed to chase away some of the earlier tension, leaving behind a cozy atmosphere that felt quintessentially Christmas.

"You know," Stephanie said softly, pausing by the display case filled with colorful treats, "I think we might just pull this off after all."

Barking Up The Wrong Bakery

Stephanie's eyes darted around the bakery, taking in the scattered ingredients and half-finished preparations. The relief of restored power was quickly replaced by a renewed sense of urgency. She turned to Jack, her brow furrowing slightly.

"Okay, crisis averted, but we're still behind schedule," she said, reaching for a nearby whisk as if drawing strength from the familiar tool. "What do you think we should prioritize?"

Jack's blue eyes scanned the room, his analytical mind already at work. "Let's focus on the signature items first. The gingerbread village and those cinnamon star cookies you're famous for."

Stephanie nodded, a small smile tugging at her lips. "Good thinking. But what about the cancellations? We're down three judges for the tasting panel."

Jack ran a hand through his short dark hair, his expression thoughtful. "We could reach out to some local business owners. Maybe the bookstore owner or the coffee shop manager?"

Stephanie's warm brown eyes lit up. "That's brilliant, Jack! And I know just the person who can help us pull this off." She reached for her phone, her fingers already dialing a familiar number. "Sam will know exactly who to call. She's got connections all over town."

As the phone rang, Stephanie felt a wave of gratitude wash over her. She glanced at Jack, who was already organizing the baking sheets, and whispered, "Thank you. For everything."

Jack's usually reserved face softened, a hint of a smile playing at the corners of his mouth. "That's what partners are for, right?"

Before Stephanie could respond, a cheerful voice burst through the phone. "Stephanie, darling! What's the latest bakery emergency?"

Stephanie couldn't help but laugh at her best friend's greeting. "Sam, you're a mind reader. I need your help with the Christmas Eve Cookie Tasting..."

Stephanie's fingers flew across her phone screen, tapping out urgent messages while Jack's deep voice resonated through the bakery as he made call after call. The air was thick with the scent of vanilla and cinnamon, a stark contrast to the tension that crackled between them.

"Any luck?" Stephanie asked, glancing up from her phone, her chestnut hair escaping its messy bun.

Jack shook his head, his blue eyes reflecting frustration. "Nothing yet. The Johnsons can't make it, and Mayor Thompson is still stuck at that conference."

Stephanie's heart sank, but she forced a smile. "We'll figure it out. We have to."

She turned her attention back to her phone, firing off another text. The clock on the wall seemed to tick louder with each passing second, a constant reminder of their dwindling time.

"Wait," Jack said suddenly, his voice tinged with excitement. "What about Carol from the flower shop? She's got quite the palate."

Stephanie's eyes lit up. "Jack, you're a genius! I'll call her right now."

As she dialed, Jack moved closer, his warmth a comforting presence beside her. Stephanie could smell his cologne, a subtle mix of pine and citrus that reminded her of winter mornings.

"Carol? Hi, it's Stephanie from Sugar & Spice. I have a huge favor to ask..."

While Stephanie chatted, Jack's phone buzzed. He answered, his voice low and measured. "Hello? Yes, this is Jack Carter. Oh, Mr. Davis, thank you for getting back to me..."

They worked in tandem, their voices overlapping, creating a symphony of determination. Stephanie felt a flutter in her chest as she caught Jack's eye, his small nod of encouragement spurring her on.

As she hung up, Stephanie let out a sigh of relief. "Carol's in. How about you?"

Jack's lips curved into a rare smile. "Mr. Davis from the hardware store is on board too. We might just pull this off, Stephanie."

She allowed herself a moment of hope, but the ticking clock quickly brought her back to reality. "We still need one more judge, and we haven't even started on the last-minute decorations."

Jack placed a reassuring hand on her shoulder, his touch sending a shiver down her spine. "One step at a time, Stephanie. We've got this."

She nodded, drawing strength from his calm demeanor. "You're right. Let's keep going. This Christmas Eve Cookie Tasting is going to be unforgettable, come hell or high water."

With renewed determination, they dove back into their phones, the race against time more urgent than ever.

Stephanie's fingers flew over her phone's keypad, her heart racing as she sent out another text. The scent of cinnamon and nutmeg still lingered in the air, a reminder of the mountains of cookies waiting to be judged. She glanced up at Jack, who was pacing near the window, his brow furrowed in concentration as he spoke quietly into his phone.

"Yes, that's right. We'd be honored if you could join us," Jack was saying, his usually reserved tone tinged with enthusiasm. "Your expertise would be invaluable."

Stephanie felt a surge of admiration for Jack's dedication. Despite his initial reluctance, he'd thrown himself into saving the event with as much passion as she had. She caught his eye and mouthed, "Any luck?"

Jack held up a finger, listening intently to the person on the other end of the line. After a moment, a smile broke across his face. "Wonderful! We'll see you tomorrow evening then. Thank you so much."

As he hung up, Stephanie couldn't contain her excitement. "Did we get our final judge?"

Jack nodded, his blue eyes twinkling. "Chef Ramirez from the culinary school in the next town over. He's excited to participate."

Stephanie let out a squeal of delight and, without thinking, threw her arms around Jack. He stiffened for a moment before relaxing into the embrace, his arms wrapping around her waist.

"We did it," Stephanie whispered, her face buried in his chest. She could feel the steady beat of his heart, smell the faint scent of his cologne mingled with the bakery's sweet aromas.

Jack pulled back slightly, looking down at her with a soft expression. "We're not out of the woods yet, but we're getting there. Your determination is... inspiring, Stephanie."

She felt a blush creep up her cheeks. "I couldn't have done it without you, Jack. We make a pretty good team."

"That we do," he agreed, a hint of something more in his voice.

As they reluctantly stepped apart, Stephanie's gaze fell on the clock. "Oh! We still need to finish the decorations. The tinsel isn't going to hang itself."

Jack chuckled, reaching for a box of ornaments. "Lead the way, Christmas cookie queen. I'm at your service."

With renewed energy, they set about transforming the bakery into a winter wonderland. As Stephanie watched Jack carefully hanging a delicate glass snowflake, she felt a warm glow of hope. Despite all the setbacks, the Christmas Eve Cookie Tasting was coming together, and with it, perhaps something even sweeter was blossoming between them.

Stephanie's heart fluttered as she watched Jack hang the last strand of twinkling lights around the bakery's front window. The soft glow illuminated his face, casting a warm radiance that made her breath catch.

"What do you think?" Jack asked, turning to her with a hopeful smile. "Festive enough?"

Stephanie nodded, her eyes sparkling. "It's perfect. The whole place looks like a Christmas card come to life."

She inhaled deeply, savoring the mingled scents of cinnamon, vanilla, and fresh pine from the wreath on the door. The bakery had transformed into a cozy haven, ready to welcome the town for tomorrow's event.

"I can't believe we pulled it off," Stephanie mused, her voice tinged with wonder. "A few hours ago, I thought everything was ruined."

Jack stepped closer, his blue eyes fixed on hers. "You never gave up, Stephanie. That's what makes you special."

A comfortable silence fell between them, filled with unspoken possibilities. Stephanie's mind raced with thoughts of the future - not just of the event, but of her and Jack, and what might be blossoming between them.

"So," Jack said softly, breaking the spell. "What's next on the list, boss?"

Stephanie laughed, the sound like tinkling bells in the quiet bakery. "Actually, I think we've earned a break. How about some hot cocoa?"

"Sounds perfect," Jack replied, his smile warming her more than any beverage could.

As Stephanie moved towards the kitchen, she couldn't help but feel that regardless of how the Cookie Tasting turned out, she had already received the best Christmas gift she could have hoped for.

Chapter 11

The aroma of cinnamon and nutmeg wafted through Stephanie's cozy bedroom as she slowly opened her eyes, the gentle chiming of her alarm clock pulling her from dreams filled with sugar plums and gingerbread. Stretching her arms above her head, she felt a flutter of excitement in her stomach, quickly followed by a twinge of nervousness.

"Today's the day," Stephanie murmured to herself, running a hand through her tousled chestnut hair. "The Cookie Tasting event is finally here."

She swung her legs out of bed, her bare feet sinking into the plush carpet. The December chill nipped at her toes, prompting her to quickly slide them into her favorite pair of fuzzy reindeer slippers. As she padded towards the window, Stephanie's mind raced with all the last-minute details she needed to check for the event.

Pulling back the curtains, she gasped softly at the sight that greeted her. A fresh blanket of snow covered Hollybrook, transforming the quaint town into a winter wonderland. Twinkling lights adorned the neighboring houses, their warm glow a stark contrast against the pristine white landscape.

"Oh, it's perfect," Stephanie breathed, her warm brown eyes sparkling with delight. "Just like something out of a Christmas card."

The sudden buzz of her phone on the nightstand startled her from her reverie. Stephanie's heart skipped a beat as she saw Jack's name flashing on the screen. A smile tugged at her lips as she answered, "Good morning, Jack. You're up early."

"Hey, Stephanie," Jack's deep voice came through, a hint of something Stephanie couldn't quite place coloring his tone. "I hope I didn't wake you."

"Not at all," Stephanie replied, twirling a lock of hair around her finger. "I was just admiring the snow. It's beautiful out there."

There was a pause on the other end of the line, and Stephanie's brow furrowed slightly. "Jack? Is everything okay?"

"Stephanie, I... I got a call last night," Jack began, his words measured and careful. "It was from my old editor in New York. They've offered me a job."

Stephanie's breath caught in her throat, her free hand gripping the windowsill tightly. "Oh," she managed, her mind whirling with a mix of emotions she couldn't quite sort out. "That's... that's big news, Jack."

"Yeah, it is," Jack agreed, his voice softening. "I wanted you to be the first to know. I haven't made any decisions yet, but..."

Stephanie closed her eyes, willing her voice to remain steady. "Of course. It's a lot to think about, I'm sure."

As Jack continued to speak, Stephanie's gaze drifted to the snow-covered streets below, the idyllic scene now feeling a world away from the turmoil in her heart. She listened intently, trying to focus on Jack's words rather than the growing knot in her stomach.

"We'll talk more later, okay?" Jack's voice brought her attention back to the conversation. "Good luck with the event today. I know you'll knock it out of the park."

"Thanks, Jack," Stephanie replied, managing a small smile despite the uncertainty swirling within her. "I'll see you there?"

"Wouldn't miss it for the world," Jack assured her before ending the call.

Stephanie stood there for a moment, phone still pressed to her ear, as the weight of Jack's news settled over her. With a deep breath, she squared her shoulders and turned towards her closet.

"Okay, Stephanie," she said to herself, determination creeping into her voice. "You've got cookies to bake and an event to run. Time to get to work."

As she pulled out her favorite Christmas sweater, Stephanie pushed her worries about Jack's news to the back of her mind. Today was about spreading joy through her baking, and she was determined to make it a success, no matter what the future might hold.

Stephanie's hands trembled as she set her phone down on the nightstand, the cheerful jingle of her holiday ringtone now a stark contrast to the heavy silence that filled her cozy bedroom. The warm glow of Christmas lights strung along her window frame seemed to dim, mirroring the sudden shift in her mood.

"New York?" she whispered to herself, her voice barely audible over the gentle hum of the heater. The scent of cinnamon and vanilla that usually brought her comfort now made her stomach churn.

Stephanie sank onto the edge of her bed, her fingers absentmindedly tracing the snowflake pattern on her quilt. She tried to process Jack's words, but they swirled in her mind like a blizzard, refusing to settle.

"It's a great opportunity," she murmured, echoing Jack's enthusiasm. But the words felt hollow, leaving a bitter taste in her mouth.

She glanced at the framed photo on her bedside table - a snapshot of her and Jack at the town's tree lighting ceremony, both grinning widely, cheeks flushed from the cold and the warmth of newfound affection. The memory, once cherished, now felt like a cruel joke.

"Of course he'll take it," Stephanie said, her voice cracking. She stood up abruptly, pacing the room. "Why wouldn't he? It's everything he left behind in New York. The prestige, the excitement, the..." She trailed off, unable to finish the thought.

The tinkling of sleigh bells from a passing car outside made Stephanie flinch. The sound, once magical, now seemed to mock her naive belief in holiday romance. She wrapped her arms around herself, suddenly feeling cold despite the cozy warmth of her room.

"I should have known better," she whispered, blinking back tears. "A big-city food critic and a small-town baker? It sounds like the plot of a cheesy Christmas movie."

Stephanie's gaze fell on her cookie cutters, neatly arranged on her dresser. The sight of them, usually a source of joy and inspiration, now filled her with a mix of determination and melancholy.

"The show must go on," she said firmly, straightening her shoulders. "Cookie Tasting event or not, broken heart or not, Hollybrook is counting on me."

With a deep breath, Stephanie reached for her apron, the familiar texture grounding her. As she tied it around her waist, she couldn't help but wonder if this would be the last Christmas she'd spend baking alongside Jack, their laughter mingling with the scent of freshly baked cookies.

Stephanie shook her head, forcing a smile onto her face as she descended the stairs to her bakery. The warm, comforting aroma of cinnamon and vanilla enveloped her, a stark contrast to the emotional turmoil swirling within.

"Alright, Sugar & Spice," she murmured, flipping on the lights. "Let's make some magic."

As she began laying out ingredients, the bell above the door chimed. Stephanie's heart skipped a beat, but it was only Mrs. Winters, her elderly neighbor.

"Good morning, dear!" Mrs. Winters chirped. "I brought you some fresh eggs from my hens. Thought they might come in handy for your big event."

Stephanie mustered a cheerful tone. "That's so thoughtful of you! These will be perfect for the snickerdoodles."

As she accepted the basket, Stephanie's mind wandered. Would Jack's sophisticated New York palate even appreciate her homey snickerdoodles anymore?

"Are you alright, Stephanie?" Mrs. Winters asked, concern etching her wrinkled face. "You seem a bit... distracted."

Stephanie forced a laugh, reaching for her mixing bowl. "Oh, just pre-event jitters. You know how it is."

As Mrs. Winters chatted about her grandchildren's upcoming visit, Stephanie mechanically began measuring flour. Her hands knew the motions, even as her heart ached. She couldn't help but wonder if every sweet moment with Jack had been nothing more than a sugar-coated illusion, destined to crumble like the cookies she was preparing.

Stephanie's shoulders sagged as Mrs. Winters left, the weight of her emotions finally crashing down. She leaned against the counter, fighting back tears, when the bell chimed again. This time, it was her sister, Olivia, bustling in with a flurry of scarves and tinsel.

"Stephanie! I brought reinforcements for decorating!" Olivia exclaimed, then paused, taking in Stephanie's expression. "Oh, sweetie. What's wrong?"

The dam broke. Stephanie's voice quavered as she explained Jack's job offer and her fears. Olivia listened, her arms around her sister, the scent of her peppermint lotion mingling with the bakery's sweetness.

"Stephanie Fields," Olivia said firmly, holding Stephanie at arm's length. "You are the strongest, most talented woman I know. If anyone can make this work, it's you."

Stephanie sniffled, managing a wobbly smile. "You really think so?"

"I know so," Olivia affirmed, squeezing Stephanie's hands. "Now, let's make this event shine brighter than the star on top of the town Christmas tree!"

Warmth spread through Stephanie's chest, not unlike the heat from her ovens. She straightened, wiping her eyes. "You're right. Cookie Tasting or heartbreak, I'm going to give this my all."

As they hung twinkling lights and arranged cookie platters, Stephanie's determination grew. She might lose Jack, but she wouldn't lose herself or disappoint her community.

"Hand me that garland," Stephanie instructed, her voice steady. "We're going to make this place look like Santa's workshop exploded in the best way possible."

Olivia grinned, passing the sparkling decoration. "That's the Stephanie I know and love."

As Stephanie climbed the stepladder, she whispered to herself, "Sugar & Spice will shine today, come what may."

The tinkling of the bakery's bell announced Samantha's arrival, her blonde curls bouncing as she bustled in, arms laden with bags. "Stephanie, sweetie! I brought reinforcements!"

Stephanie climbed down from the ladder, her heart lifting at the sight of her best friend. "Sam, you're a lifesaver!"

Samantha set down her bags, revealing an assortment of festive napkins and cookie boxes. She enveloped Stephanie in a warm hug, the scent of her cinnamon perfume wrapping around them both. "How are you holding up, hon?"

Stephanie's smile faltered. "I'm... managing. It's just—"

"Jack?" Samantha guessed, her blue eyes full of understanding.

Stephanie nodded, her throat tight. "I don't know what to do, Sam. What if he leaves?"

Samantha guided Stephanie to a nearby table, their hands intertwined. "Listen to me, Em. Whatever happens, you're going to be okay. You're the heart of this town, and we all love you."

"But what if—"

"No 'what ifs'," Samantha interrupted gently. "You've got this event to focus on, and it's going to be amazing. Everything else will work itself out."

Stephanie took a deep breath, the sugary aroma of freshly baked cookies filling her lungs. "You really think so?"

"I know so," Samantha affirmed, squeezing Stephanie's hand. "Now, let's get this place ready to dazzle!"

As Samantha bustled off to arrange centerpieces, Stephanie found herself alone for a moment. She leaned against the counter, her fingers tracing the worn wood grain. Her mind wandered to Jack, to their first meeting right here in this very spot.

"Who knew a grumpy food critic could become so important to me?" Stephanie mused silently, a bittersweet smile playing on her lips. She remembered their playful banter over cookie flavors, the way his stern expression had softened when he'd tasted her gingerbread.

Stephanie closed her eyes, recalling the warmth of Jack's hand on hers as they'd strolled through the town's twinkling Christmas light display. The memory of their almost-kiss under the mistletoe sent a shiver down her spine.

"We've come so far," Stephanie whispered to herself. "But where do we go from here?"

Stephanie shook herself from her reverie, the distant chiming of the town clock reminding her of the ticking minutes. With renewed focus, she tied her chestnut hair into a messy bun and rolled up her sleeves, revealing arms dusted with a fine layer of flour.

"Alright, Sugar & Spice," she murmured to the empty bakery, "let's make some magic."

The kitchen soon filled with the rhythmic sound of Stephanie's rolling pin, punctuated by the soft puffs of powdered sugar as she dusted each cookie. The sweet scent of vanilla and cinnamon wafted through the air, mingling with the comforting aroma of melting chocolate.

As she worked, Stephanie poured her conflicting emotions into every swirl of frosting, every sprinkle of crushed peppermint. Her brows furrowed in concentration as she meticulously arranged cookie platters, each one a work of art.

"These snowflake cookies need just a touch more sparkle," Stephanie muttered, reaching for the edible glitter.

The jingle of the bakery's bell startled her, and she called out, "We're not open yet!"

"Not even for your mother?" came a familiar, warm voice.

Stephanie's head snapped up, her eyes meeting the gentle gaze of Margaret Fields. "Mom? What are you doing here?"

Maggie stepped into the kitchen, her eyes twinkling as she took in the festive chaos. "I thought you might need an extra pair of hands... and maybe an ear to listen."

Stephanie's lower lip trembled slightly as she set down her piping bag. "Oh, Mom," she whispered, suddenly feeling like a little girl again.

Maggie enveloped her daughter in a hug that smelled of home – a mix of lavender and freshly baked bread. "Now, sweetheart," she said, pulling back to look Stephanie in the eye, "tell me what's troubling that beautiful heart of yours."

Stephanie's words tumbled out in a rush, her hands gesticulating as she spoke about Jack, the job offer, and her fears. Maggie listened patiently, her weathered hands working alongside Stephanie's, expertly forming cookie dough into perfect circles.

When Stephanie finally fell silent, Maggie spoke softly. "You know, dear, the best recipes aren't always the ones that follow every rule. Sometimes, it's the unexpected pinch of this or dash of that that makes them truly special."

Stephanie frowned, confusion evident in her warm brown eyes. "What do you mean, Mom?"

Maggie smiled, pressing a warm cookie into Stephanie's flour-dusted hand. "I mean that life, like baking, isn't always about following a set path. It's about trusting your instincts, taking risks, and most importantly, following your heart."

Stephanie stood in the center of her bustling bakery, the words of her mother echoing in her mind. The air was thick with the scent of cinnamon and vanilla, mingling with the fresh pine from the garland adorning the windows. She took a deep breath, savoring the comforting aroma that had always been her anchor.

"Alright, team," Stephanie called out, her voice steady despite the turmoil in her heart. "Let's make this Cookie Tasting event one for the books!"

Her staff cheered, their enthusiasm infectious. Stephanie felt a smile tugging at her lips as she surveyed the scene before her. Trays of colorful cookies lined every available surface, each one a testament to her creativity and passion.

As she piped delicate snowflakes onto a batch of sugar cookies, Stephanie's mind wandered to Jack. The ache in her chest was still there, but it was overshadowed by a fierce determination. "I can do this," she murmured to herself. "With or without him."

Just then, the bakery's bell chimed, and a gust of crisp winter air swept in. Stephanie looked up, her heart skipping a beat before she realized it was just another eager customer.

"Welcome to Sugar & Spice," she called out warmly, pushing thoughts of Jack aside. "Ready to taste some Christmas magic?"

As she turned back to her work, Stephanie took another deep breath. The familiar scents and sounds of her beloved bakery wrapped around her like a cozy blanket, reminding her of all she had accomplished. With a small nod to herself, she squared her shoulders and dove back into her preparations, ready to face whatever the day might bring.

Stephanie's gaze drifted to the frosted window, where twinkling lights from neighboring shops cast a warm glow on the freshly fallen snow. The sight reminded her of the magical evening she and Jack had spent strolling through town, their gloved hands intertwined.

"No use dwelling on what might have been," she whispered, her breath creating a small cloud in the chilly air. She turned back to the bustling bakery, the clatter of mixing bowls and laughter of her staff filling the air.

As she reached for a tray of gingerbread men, the rich aroma of cinnamon and molasses enveloping her, Stephanie made a decision. "I'm going to cherish every moment we have left," she said softly, a bittersweet smile playing on her lips.

Just then, Sam appeared at her side, flour dusting her apron. "Hey, Em. You okay?"

Stephanie nodded, her eyes shining with unshed tears and newfound resolve. "You know what, Sam? I am. Whatever happens with Jack, I'm grateful for the time we've shared."

Sam squeezed her arm. "That's my girl. Now, let's knock their socks off with these cookies!"

As they worked side by side, Stephanie's heart felt lighter. She may not know what the future held, but she was determined to savor every sweet moment of the present, just like the delectable treats they were creating.

"Life's too short for regrets," Stephanie mused, carefully placing a tray of star-shaped cookies into the oven. "I'm going to make every second count, starting now."

Chapter 12

The aroma of cinnamon and nutmeg wafted through Stephanie's cozy bedroom as she slowly opened her eyes, the gentle chiming of her alarm clock pulling her from dreams filled with sugar plums and gingerbread. Stretching her arms above her head, she felt a flutter of excitement in her stomach, quickly followed by a twinge of nervousness.

"Today's the day," Stephanie murmured to herself, running a hand through her tousled chestnut hair. "The Cookie Tasting event is finally here."

She swung her legs out of bed, her bare feet sinking into the plush carpet. The December chill nipped at her toes, prompting her to quickly slide them into her favorite pair of fuzzy reindeer slippers. As she padded towards the window, Stephanie's mind raced with all the last-minute details she needed to check for the event.

Pulling back the curtains, she gasped softly at the sight that greeted her. A fresh blanket of snow covered Hollybrook, transforming the quaint town into a winter wonderland. Twinkling lights adorned the neighboring houses, their warm glow a stark contrast against the pristine white landscape.

"Oh, it's perfect," Stephanie breathed, her warm brown eyes sparkling with delight. "Just like something out of a Christmas card."

The sudden buzz of her phone on the nightstand startled her from her reverie. Stephanie's heart skipped a beat as she saw Jack's name flashing on the screen. A smile tugged at her lips as she answered, "Good morning, Jack. You're up early."

"Hey, Stephanie," Jack's deep voice came through, a hint of something Stephanie couldn't quite place coloring his tone. "I hope I didn't wake you."

"Not at all," Stephanie replied, twirling a lock of hair around her finger. "I was just admiring the snow. It's beautiful out there."

There was a pause on the other end of the line, and Stephanie's brow furrowed slightly. "Jack? Is everything okay?"

"Stephanie, I... I got a call last night," Jack began, his words measured and careful. "It was from my old editor in New York. They've offered me a job."

Stephanie's breath caught in her throat, her free hand gripping the windowsill tightly. "Oh," she managed, her mind whirling with a mix of emotions she couldn't quite sort out. "That's... that's big news, Jack."

"Yeah, it is," Jack agreed, his voice softening. "I wanted you to be the first to know. I haven't made any decisions yet, but..."

Stephanie closed her eyes, willing her voice to remain steady. "Of course. It's a lot to think about, I'm sure."

As Jack continued to speak, Stephanie's gaze drifted to the snow-covered streets below, the idyllic scene now feeling a world away from the turmoil in her heart. She listened intently, trying to focus on Jack's words rather than the growing knot in her stomach.

"We'll talk more later, okay?" Jack's voice brought her attention back to the conversation. "Good luck with the event today. I know you'll knock it out of the park."

"Thanks, Jack," Stephanie replied, managing a small smile despite the uncertainty swirling within her. "I'll see you there?"

"Wouldn't miss it for the world," Jack assured her before ending the call.

Stephanie stood there for a moment, phone still pressed to her ear, as the weight of Jack's news settled over her. With a deep breath, she squared her shoulders and turned towards her closet.

"Okay, Stephanie," she said to herself, determination creeping into her voice. "You've got cookies to bake and an event to run. Time to get to work."

As she pulled out her favorite Christmas sweater, Stephanie pushed her worries about Jack's news to the back of her mind. Today was about spreading joy through her baking, and she was determined to make it a success, no matter what the future might hold.

Stephanie's hands trembled as she set her phone down on the nightstand, the cheerful jingle of her holiday ringtone now a stark contrast to the heavy silence that filled her cozy bedroom. The warm glow of Christmas lights strung along her window frame seemed to dim, mirroring the sudden shift in her mood.

"New York?" she whispered to herself, her voice barely audible over the gentle hum of the heater. The scent of cinnamon and vanilla that usually brought her comfort now made her stomach churn.

Stephanie sank onto the edge of her bed, her fingers absentmindedly tracing the snowflake pattern on her quilt. She tried to process Jack's words, but they swirled in her mind like a blizzard, refusing to settle.

"It's a great opportunity," she murmured, echoing Jack's enthusiasm. But the words felt hollow, leaving a bitter taste in her mouth.

She glanced at the framed photo on her bedside table - a snapshot of her and Jack at the town's tree lighting ceremony, both grinning widely, cheeks flushed from the cold and the warmth of newfound affection. The memory, once cherished, now felt like a cruel joke.

"Of course he'll take it," Stephanie said, her voice cracking. She stood up abruptly, pacing the room. "Why wouldn't he? It's everything he left behind in New York. The prestige, the excitement, the..." She trailed off, unable to finish the thought.

The tinkling of sleigh bells from a passing car outside made Stephanie flinch. The sound, once magical, now seemed to mock her naive belief in holiday romance. She wrapped her arms around herself, suddenly feeling cold despite the cozy warmth of her room.

"I should have known better," she whispered, blinking back tears. "A big-city food critic and a small-town baker? It sounds like the plot of a cheesy Christmas movie."

Stephanie's gaze fell on her cookie cutters, neatly arranged on her dresser. The sight of them, usually a source of joy and inspiration, now filled her with a mix of determination and melancholy.

"The show must go on," she said firmly, straightening her shoulders. "Cookie Tasting event or not, broken heart or not, Hollybrook is counting on me."

With a deep breath, Stephanie reached for her apron, the familiar texture grounding her. As she tied it around her waist, she couldn't help but wonder if this would be the last Christmas she'd spend baking alongside Jack, their laughter mingling with the scent of freshly baked cookies.

Stephanie shook her head, forcing a smile onto her face as she descended the stairs to her bakery. The warm, comforting aroma of cinnamon and vanilla enveloped her, a stark contrast to the emotional turmoil swirling within.

"Alright, Sugar & Spice," she murmured, flipping on the lights. "Let's make some magic."

As she began laying out ingredients, the bell above the door chimed. Stephanie's heart skipped a beat, but it was only Mrs. Winters, her elderly neighbor.

"Good morning, dear!" Mrs. Winters chirped. "I brought you some fresh eggs from my hens. Thought they might come in handy for your big event."

Stephanie mustered a cheerful tone. "That's so thoughtful of you! These will be perfect for the snickerdoodles."

As she accepted the basket, Stephanie's mind wandered. Would Jack's sophisticated New York palate even appreciate her homey snickerdoodles anymore?

"Are you alright, Stephanie?" Mrs. Winters asked, concern etching her wrinkled face. "You seem a bit... distracted."

Stephanie forced a laugh, reaching for her mixing bowl. "Oh, just pre-event jitters. You know how it is."

As Mrs. Winters chatted about her grandchildren's upcoming visit, Stephanie mechanically began measuring flour. Her hands knew the motions, even as her heart ached. She couldn't help but wonder if every sweet moment with Jack had been nothing more than a sugar-coated illusion, destined to crumble like the cookies she was preparing.

Stephanie's shoulders sagged as Mrs. Winters left, the weight of her emotions finally crashing down. She leaned against the counter, fighting back tears, when the bell chimed again. This time, it was her sister, Olivia, bustling in with a flurry of scarves and tinsel.

"Stephanie! I brought reinforcements for decorating!" Olivia exclaimed, then paused, taking in Stephanie's expression. "Oh, sweetie. What's wrong?"

The dam broke. Stephanie's voice quavered as she explained Jack's job offer and her fears. Olivia listened, her arms around her sister, the scent of her peppermint lotion mingling with the bakery's sweetness.

"Stephanie Fields," Olivia said firmly, holding Stephanie at arm's length. "You are the strongest, most talented woman I know. If anyone can make this work, it's you."

Stephanie sniffled, managing a wobbly smile. "You really think so?"

"I know so," Olivia affirmed, squeezing Stephanie's hands. "Now, let's make this event shine brighter than the star on top of the town Christmas tree!"

Warmth spread through Stephanie's chest, not unlike the heat from her ovens. She straightened, wiping her eyes. "You're right. Cookie Tasting or heartbreak, I'm going to give this my all."

As they hung twinkling lights and arranged cookie platters, Stephanie's determination grew. She might lose Jack, but she wouldn't lose herself or disappoint her community.

"Hand me that garland," Stephanie instructed, her voice steady. "We're going to make this place look like Santa's workshop exploded in the best way possible."

Olivia grinned, passing the sparkling decoration. "That's the Stephanie I know and love."

As Stephanie climbed the stepladder, she whispered to herself, "Sugar & Spice will shine today, come what may."

The tinkling of the bakery's bell announced Samantha's arrival, her blonde curls bouncing as she bustled in, arms laden with bags. "Stephanie, sweetie! I brought reinforcements!"

Stephanie climbed down from the ladder, her heart lifting at the sight of her best friend. "Sam, you're a lifesaver!"

Samantha set down her bags, revealing an assortment of festive napkins and cookie boxes. She enveloped Stephanie in a warm hug, the scent of her cinnamon perfume wrapping around them both. "How are you holding up, hon?"

Stephanie's smile faltered. "I'm... managing. It's just—"

"Jack?" Samantha guessed, her blue eyes full of understanding.

Stephanie nodded, her throat tight. "I don't know what to do, Sam. What if he leaves?"

Samantha guided Stephanie to a nearby table, their hands intertwined. "Listen to me, Em. Whatever happens, you're going to be okay. You're the heart of this town, and we all love you."

"But what if—"

"No 'what ifs'," Samantha interrupted gently. "You've got this event to focus on, and it's going to be amazing. Everything else will work itself out."

Stephanie took a deep breath, the sugary aroma of freshly baked cookies filling her lungs. "You really think so?"

"I know so," Samantha affirmed, squeezing Stephanie's hand. "Now, let's get this place ready to dazzle!"

As Samantha bustled off to arrange centerpieces, Stephanie found herself alone for a moment. She leaned against the counter, her fingers tracing the worn wood grain. Her mind wandered to Jack, to their first meeting right here in this very spot.

"Who knew a grumpy food critic could become so important to me?" Stephanie mused silently, a bittersweet smile playing on her lips. She remembered their playful banter over cookie flavors, the way his stern expression had softened when he'd tasted her gingerbread.

Stephanie closed her eyes, recalling the warmth of Jack's hand on hers as they'd strolled through the town's twinkling Christmas light display. The memory of their almost-kiss under the mistletoe sent a shiver down her spine.

"We've come so far," Stephanie whispered to herself. "But where do we go from here?"

Stephanie shook herself from her reverie, the distant chiming of the town clock reminding her of the ticking minutes. With renewed focus, she tied her chestnut hair into a messy bun and rolled up her sleeves, revealing arms dusted with a fine layer of flour.

"Alright, Sugar & Spice," she murmured to the empty bakery, "let's make some magic."

The kitchen soon filled with the rhythmic sound of Stephanie's rolling pin, punctuated by the soft puffs of powdered sugar as she dusted each cookie. The sweet scent of vanilla and cinnamon wafted through the air, mingling with the comforting aroma of melting chocolate.

As she worked, Stephanie poured her conflicting emotions into every swirl of frosting, every sprinkle of crushed peppermint. Her brows furrowed in concentration as she meticulously arranged cookie platters, each one a work of art.

"These snowflake cookies need just a touch more sparkle," Stephanie muttered, reaching for the edible glitter.

The jingle of the bakery's bell startled her, and she called out, "We're not open yet!"

"Not even for your mother?" came a familiar, warm voice.

Stephanie's head snapped up, her eyes meeting the gentle gaze of Margaret Fields. "Mom? What are you doing here?"

Maggie stepped into the kitchen, her eyes twinkling as she took in the festive chaos. "I thought you might need an extra pair of hands... and maybe an ear to listen."

Stephanie's lower lip trembled slightly as she set down her piping bag. "Oh, Mom," she whispered, suddenly feeling like a little girl again.

Maggie enveloped her daughter in a hug that smelled of home – a mix of lavender and freshly baked bread. "Now, sweetheart," she said, pulling back to look Stephanie in the eye, "tell me what's troubling that beautiful heart of yours."

Stephanie's words tumbled out in a rush, her hands gesticulating as she spoke about Jack, the job offer, and her fears. Maggie listened patiently, her weathered hands working alongside Stephanie's, expertly forming cookie dough into perfect circles.

When Stephanie finally fell silent, Maggie spoke softly. "You know, dear, the best recipes aren't always the ones that follow every rule. Sometimes, it's the unexpected pinch of this or dash of that that makes them truly special."

Stephanie frowned, confusion evident in her warm brown eyes. "What do you mean, Mom?"

Maggie smiled, pressing a warm cookie into Stephanie's flour-dusted hand. "I mean that life, like baking, isn't always about following a set path. It's about trusting your instincts, taking risks, and most importantly, following your heart."

Stephanie stood in the center of her bustling bakery, the words of her mother echoing in her mind. The air was thick with the scent of cinnamon and vanilla, mingling with the fresh pine from the garland adorning the windows. She took a deep breath, savoring the comforting aroma that had always been her anchor.

"Alright, team," Stephanie called out, her voice steady despite the turmoil in her heart. "Let's make this Cookie Tasting event one for the books!"

Her staff cheered, their enthusiasm infectious. Stephanie felt a smile tugging at her lips as she surveyed the scene before her. Trays of colorful cookies lined every available surface, each one a testament to her creativity and passion.

As she piped delicate snowflakes onto a batch of sugar cookies, Stephanie's mind wandered to Jack. The ache in her chest was still there, but it was overshadowed by a fierce determination. "I can do this," she murmured to herself. "With or without him."

Just then, the bakery's bell chimed, and a gust of crisp winter air swept in. Stephanie looked up, her heart skipping a beat before she realized it was just another eager customer.

"Welcome to Sugar & Spice," she called out warmly, pushing thoughts of Jack aside. "Ready to taste some Christmas magic?"

As she turned back to her work, Stephanie took another deep breath. The familiar scents and sounds of her beloved bakery wrapped around her like a cozy blanket, reminding her of all she had accomplished. With a small nod to herself, she squared her shoulders and dove back into her preparations, ready to face whatever the day might bring.

Stephanie's gaze drifted to the frosted window, where twinkling lights from neighboring shops cast a warm glow on the freshly fallen snow. The sight reminded her of the magical evening she and Jack had spent strolling through town, their gloved hands intertwined.

"No use dwelling on what might have been," she whispered, her breath creating a small cloud in the chilly air. She turned back to the bustling bakery, the clatter of mixing bowls and laughter of her staff filling the air.

As she reached for a tray of gingerbread men, the rich aroma of cinnamon and molasses enveloping her, Stephanie made a decision. "I'm going to cherish every moment we have left," she said softly, a bittersweet smile playing on her lips.

Just then, Sam appeared at her side, flour dusting her apron. "Hey, Em. You okay?"

Stephanie nodded, her eyes shining with unshed tears and newfound resolve. "You know what, Sam? I am. Whatever happens with Jack, I'm grateful for the time we've shared."

Sam squeezed her arm. "That's my girl. Now, let's knock their socks off with these cookies!"

As they worked side by side, Stephanie's heart felt lighter. She may not know what the future held, but she was determined to savor every sweet moment of the present, just like the delectable treats they were creating.

"Life's too short for regrets," Stephanie mused, carefully placing a tray of star-shaped cookies into the oven. "I'm going to make every second count, starting now."

Chapter 13

The scent of cinnamon and vanilla lingered in the air as Stephanie closed her office door, her heart racing. Jack stood by her desk, his tall frame silhouetted against the twinkling Christmas lights adorning the window behind him. The small space seemed to crackle with unspoken tension.

"Jack, I..." Stephanie began, then faltered. She twisted her flour-dusted apron in her hands, searching for the right words. How could she possibly express the whirlwind of emotions she felt whenever he was near?

Jack took a step closer, his blue eyes intense. "Stephanie, there's something I need to tell you." His voice was low, almost a whisper.

Stephanie's breath caught in her throat. She could hear the faint strains of "White Christmas" playing in the bakery beyond, the cheerful melody a stark contrast to the heavy atmosphere in her tiny office.

"I've been thinking about us," Jack continued, running a hand through his dark hair. "About how things have changed since I came to Hollybrook."

Stephanie nodded, her chest tight. "I know what you mean. Everything feels... different now."

A moment of silence stretched between them, filled with the weight of unspoken feelings. Stephanie's gaze darted to the framed photo on her desk - her grandmother smiling in the old bakery kitchen. What would she say about this situation?

Jack cleared his throat. "I never expected to find... this... when I left New York." He gestured vaguely between them.

Stephanie's heart skipped a beat. "This?" she echoed, hardly daring to hope.

"You," Jack said softly. "Us. This connection."

Stephanie took a shaky breath, the scent of gingerbread from the kitchen mingling with Jack's subtle cologne. She wanted to reach out, to bridge the gap between them, but uncertainty held her back.

"Jack, I don't know how to say this, but..." Stephanie began, her voice trembling slightly.

Just then, a timer dinged loudly in the kitchen, making them both jump. Stephanie let out a nervous laugh, the spell of the moment temporarily broken.

"Your snickerdoodles," Jack said with a small smile, remembering her baking schedule.

Stephanie nodded, grateful for the brief reprieve. "They'll burn if I don't..."

"Go ahead," Jack said gently. "We can finish this conversation later."

As Stephanie reached for the door handle, she paused, turning back to Jack. The Christmas lights cast a warm glow on his face, highlighting the tenderness in his eyes. In that moment, surrounded by the sights and smells of her beloved bakery, Stephanie knew that whatever happened next would change everything.

Stephanie's fingers tightened on the doorknob, her heart pounding like a mixer on high speed. She turned back to face Jack, the soft glow of twinkling lights reflecting in his deep blue eyes.

"No," she said firmly, surprising herself. "The cookies can wait. This... this is more important."

Jack's eyebrows raised slightly, a mix of curiosity and anticipation crossing his face. "Stephanie, what are you—"

"I need to say this, Jack," Stephanie interrupted, her voice barely above a whisper. She took a deep breath, inhaling the comforting scent of cinnamon and vanilla that always clung to her clothes. "I've been afraid to admit it, even to myself, but being with you... it feels like coming home."

Jack's expression softened, but he remained silent, giving her space to continue.

Stephanie's hands fidgeted with the hem of her flour-dusted apron. "I know we come from different worlds. You're used to Michelin stars and fancy restaurants, and I'm just a small-town baker. But when I'm with you, none of that matters. It's like... like the perfect recipe coming together."

She closed her eyes briefly, gathering her courage. When she opened them again, she met Jack's gaze directly. "I'm scared, Jack. Scared of how much I care about you, scared of how quickly this happened. But I'm more scared of letting this chance slip away."

The silence that followed was thick with tension, broken only by the distant sound of carols drifting in from the town square. Stephanie's heart raced as she waited for Jack's response, the taste of uncertainty bitter on her tongue.

Jack's eyes widened, a mix of surprise and vulnerability flickering across his face. He took a step closer to Stephanie, the scent of his subtle cologne mingling with the bakery's sweet aromas.

"Stephanie," he began, his voice low and slightly rough with emotion. "I never expected to find... this... when I came to Hollybrook." He gestured between them, a small smile tugging at the corners of his mouth.

Stephanie's heart fluttered, hope blooming in her chest like the first flowers of spring. She watched as Jack's usual composed demeanor softened, his guard lowering.

"You're right, we're from different worlds," he continued, running a hand through his dark hair. "But being here, with you, in this charming bakery... it's shown me what really matters."

He reached out, gently taking her flour-dusted hand in his. The warmth of his touch sent a shiver down Stephanie's spine.

"You've brought color back into my life, Stephanie," Jack admitted, his blue eyes intense and sincere. "Your passion, your kindness, the way you light up this entire town... it's captivating."

Stephanie felt tears prick at the corners of her eyes, overwhelmed by the tenderness in Jack's words and the vulnerability in his expression. The soft glow of the bakery's Christmas lights cast a warm, golden hue over them both, creating an intimate cocoon in the quiet office.

Jack's thumb traced gentle circles on Stephanie's hand as he took a deep breath, his chest rising and falling with the weight of his next words. "I've fallen in love with you, Stephanie," he confessed, his voice barely above a whisper. "And I want to be with you, if you'll have me."

Stephanie's breath caught in her throat, her eyes widening at Jack's declaration. The world seemed to narrow to just the two of them, the gentle hum of the bakery's ovens fading into the background.

"Jack, I—" Stephanie started, but words failed her. Instead, she squeezed his hand, a beaming smile spreading across her face as she nodded emphatically.

A moment of profound silence fell between them, filled with unspoken promises and shared understanding. The air felt charged with possibility, like the anticipation before the first snowfall of winter. Stephanie could hear her own heartbeat, steady and sure, matching the rhythm of Jack's breathing.

They stood there, hand in hand, as the reality of their confessions settled around them like a warm, comforting blanket. The scent of cinnamon and vanilla wafted through the air, a sweet reminder of the life they could build together in this cozy corner of Hollybrook.

Stephanie's eyes met Jack's, a mixture of joy and apprehension swirling in their warm brown depths. "This won't be easy, you know," she said softly, her fingers still intertwined with his. "Running a bakery during Christmas season is... intense. There will be long hours, stressful days..."

Jack nodded, a wry smile tugging at his lips. "And I'm not exactly known for my patience with holiday crowds," he admitted, thinking back to his days as a New York food critic.

Stephanie couldn't help but chuckle, the sound like tinkling bells in the quiet office. "We're quite the pair, aren't we?"

"But that's what makes us work," Jack insisted, his blue eyes earnest. "Your passion, my practicality. We balance each other out."

Stephanie nodded, her expression growing serious. "Speaking of practicality... we need to talk about Peter Hamilton's offer."

Jack tensed slightly at the mention of the businessman's name. "What are you thinking?"

Stephanie took a deep breath, inhaling the comforting scent of freshly baked gingerbread. "I'm thinking... we should decline," she said firmly. "Sugar & Spice isn't just a bakery, Jack. It's a piece of

Hollybrook's heart. Expanding might bring in more money, but at what cost?"

Jack's eyes softened as he looked at Stephanie, seeing the determination in her face. "You're right," he agreed. "The charm of this place, the way it brings the community together... that's worth more than any franchise deal."

Stephanie beamed, relief washing over her. "So we're in agreement? We'll tell Peter thanks, but no thanks?"

Jack nodded, a mischievous glint in his eye. "Absolutely. Though I have to admit, I'm looking forward to seeing his face when we break the news. He seemed pretty confident we'd jump at the chance."

Stephanie laughed, the sound echoing off the walls of her small office. "Well, Mr. Former Food Critic, I'm sure you can find a way to let him down gently."

As their laughter subsided, Stephanie felt a surge of warmth in her chest. They had challenges ahead, no doubt, but facing them together felt right. Like the perfect recipe, all the ingredients were falling into place.

Stephanie's eyes met Jack's, and in that moment, the air between them seemed to crackle with unspoken emotion. Without a word, Jack reached out, gently taking Stephanie's flour-dusted hand in his own. His touch was warm and reassuring, sending a pleasant shiver up her arm.

"Stephanie," Jack said softly, his voice barely above a whisper, "I want you to know that I'm all in. This bakery, this town, us... it feels like home."

Stephanie's heart swelled, and she squeezed his hand in response. "I feel the same way," she murmured, her eyes glistening with unshed tears of joy.

Unable to resist any longer, Stephanie stepped forward, closing the distance between them. Jack's arms enveloped her in a tender embrace, and she nestled her head against his chest, inhaling the subtle scent of his cologne mingled with the ever-present aroma of vanilla and cinnamon that permeated the bakery.

As they held each other, Stephanie's mind drifted to the future. She imagined cozy winter evenings spent experimenting with new recipes, Jack by her side offering his culinary expertise. She pictured summer picnics in the town square, sharing slices of her famous strawberry shortcake with their friends and neighbors.

"You know," Stephanie said, her voice muffled against Jack's sweater, "I have a feeling our story is just beginning."

Jack pulled back slightly, a warm smile playing on his lips. "I couldn't agree more," he replied, his blue eyes twinkling. "And I can't wait to see what the next chapter holds."

As they stood there, bathed in the soft glow of twinkling Christmas lights that adorned Stephanie's office window, the future stretched out before them like a blank canvas, ready to be filled with love, laughter, and the sweet aroma of freshly baked happiness.

Chapter 14

The scent of cinnamon and vanilla wafted through Sugar & Spice Bakery as Stephanie reached up on her tiptoes, delicately hanging a string of twinkling lights along the exposed wooden beams. Her chestnut hair, escaping from its messy bun, tickled her cheek as she stretched.

"Jack, can you hand me that last strand?" Stephanie called over her shoulder, her warm brown eyes sparkling with anticipation.

Jack's tall frame appeared beside her, a gentle smile playing on his lips. "Here you go," he said, his deep voice tinged with amusement. "Though I think you might need a stepladder for that last bit."

Stephanie laughed, the sound as sweet as the treats surrounding them. "Are you offering to be my personal ladder, Mr. Carter?"

As Jack opened his mouth to reply, a blur of black fur darted between their legs, followed by the distinct crunch of a cookie being devoured.

"Tessa!" Stephanie exclaimed, her eyes widening as she spotted the mischievous dachshund with crumbs on her snout. "Oh no, those were for the display!"

Stephanie's heart raced as she lunged for the pup, but Tessa was too quick. The little dog's nails clicked against the polished floor as she zipped behind the counter, her tail wagging triumphantly.

Jack chuckled, his blue eyes twinkling. "I'll cut her off at the pass," he said, moving swiftly towards the other end of the bakery.

Stephanie couldn't help but smile, despite the chaos. This is exactly what the bakery needed - a little life, a little laughter. Even if it came in the form of a cookie-stealing dachshund.

"Tessa, come here, girl," Stephanie coaxed, crouching down and holding out her hand. The pup's nose twitched, clearly torn between the allure of more treats and the promise of pets.

Just as Stephanie thought she had Tessa cornered, the clever canine darted between her legs, making a beeline for the meticulously arranged cookie platters.

"Jack, she's heading your way!" Stephanie called out, her voice a mix of exasperation and amusement.

As she watched Jack make a graceful dive for the pup, narrowly missing and sending a whirlwind of flour into the air, Stephanie couldn't help but think how perfectly imperfect this moment was. It was exactly the kind of warmth and joy she'd always wanted to create in her bakery.

"You know," Stephanie said, brushing flour off Jack's shoulder as he stood up, Tessa still eluding their grasp, "I think this might be the most fun I've had decorating for an event."

Jack's eyes softened as he looked at her, a slow smile spreading across his face. "Even with a four-legged cookie thief on the loose?"

"Especially with a four-legged cookie thief on the loose," Stephanie replied, her heart skipping a beat at the warmth in Jack's gaze.

As they turned to continue their pursuit of the playful pup, Stephanie couldn't help but feel that this Christmas Eve was shaping up to be something truly special.

Stephanie's laughter echoed through the bakery as she and Jack rounded the corner, hot on Tessa's tail. The mischievous dachshund's nails clicked against the polished floor, her sleek black body a blur as she darted between tables.

"Tessa, you little rascal!" Jack called out, his usually composed demeanor cracking with amusement.

Stephanie's heart raced, not just from the chase but from the sheer joy of the moment. She reached out, fingers grazing Tessa's fur, when suddenly—

CRASH!

Time seemed to slow as Stephanie's hip bumped a nearby table, sending a tray of carefully decorated gingerbread men tumbling to the floor. The cookies slid across the smooth surface, creating a domino effect that toppled platters on adjacent tables.

"Oh no!" Stephanie gasped, watching in horror as her creations scattered across the floor.

Jack skidded to a halt beside her, his blue eyes wide with surprise. For a moment, they stood frozen, surveying the chaos of fallen cookies and upturned platters. Then, as if on cue, they both burst into laughter.

"Well," Jack chuckled, running a hand through his dark hair, "I guess that's one way to rearrange the display."

Stephanie felt tears of mirth forming in her eyes. "Oh, Jack," she managed between giggles, "what are we going to do?"

As their laughter subsided, Stephanie's gaze met Jack's, and she felt a warmth spread through her chest. There was something about his presence that made even disasters feel manageable.

"We'll clean it up together," Jack said softly, giving her arm a gentle squeeze. "Besides, I think I know a certain four-legged friend who'd be more than happy to help dispose of the evidence."

As if on cue, Tessa trotted over, tail wagging, looking entirely too pleased with herself.

"You little troublemaker," Stephanie cooed, unable to stay mad at the adorable pup.

They set about cleaning up the mess, working side by side in comfortable silence. Stephanie couldn't help but marvel at how natural it felt, how perfectly Jack seemed to fit into her world.

As they finished tidying up, the bakery's bell chimed, signaling the arrival of the first guests. Stephanie straightened up, smoothing down her flour-dusted apron and tucking a stray strand of hair behind her ear.

"Ready?" Jack asked, his calm demeanor a soothing contrast to her nervous excitement.

Stephanie took a deep breath, inhaling the comforting scents of cinnamon, vanilla, and freshly baked cookies that filled the air. "Ready," she replied with a confident smile.

Together, they moved to greet their guests, the bakery now alive with the soft glow of twinkling lights and the warmth of Christmas cheer. As Stephanie welcomed the first group of attendees, offering them a tray of her signature sugar cookies, she couldn't help but feel that this night was going to be truly magical.

Stephanie chatted with Mrs. Henderson, a regular customer who always had a kind word to share. "I simply must know the secret to these gingerbread cookies, dear," Mrs. Henderson said, taking another bite. "They're absolutely divine!"

Stephanie laughed, a warm sound that filled the cozy bakery. "Well, I can't give away all my secrets, but I will say that a dash of cardamom makes all the difference."

As she spoke, Stephanie's gaze drifted to Jack, who was across the room discussing the finer points of shortbread with Mr. Peterson. She felt a flutter in her chest, watching him gesticulate enthusiastically, his blue eyes alight with passion.

"Your young man there seems to know his way around a cookie sheet," Mrs. Henderson remarked with a knowing wink.

Stephanie felt her cheeks warm. "Oh, Jack's not... we're just..." she stammered, suddenly flustered. "He's been a wonderful help with the bakery," she finished lamely, inwardly cringing at her awkward response.

Just then, a flash of black fur caught her eye. Tessa, seizing her moment, had wriggled free from her temporary enclosure and was making a beeline for the cookie display.

"Oh no," Stephanie muttered under her breath. She locked eyes with Jack across the room, seeing her own mix of amusement and exasperation mirrored in his expression.

With a quick "Excuse me," to Mrs. Henderson, Stephanie began weaving through the crowd, trying to intercept the mischievous dachshund. She could see Jack doing the same from the other side of the bakery.

"Tessa, you little rascal," Stephanie called softly, trying not to draw too much attention. She dodged around a group of carolers, the scent of peppermint and chocolate growing stronger as she neared the cookie display. "Jack, she's heading your way!"

Stephanie lunged forward, her fingers just grazing Tessa's silky fur as the nimble dachshund darted between her legs. "Gotcha!" she exclaimed triumphantly, only to realize she was grasping at air. Tessa had slipped away again, this time heading straight for the hot cocoa station.

"Jack, she's—" Stephanie's warning was cut short by a resounding crash. Tessa had collided with the marshmallow jar, sending fluffy white puffs cascading across the floor like edible snowflakes.

Stephanie's hand flew to her mouth, stifling a giggle as she met Jack's gaze. His eyes crinkled with amusement, a rare, genuine smile spreading across his face.

"Well," Jack chuckled, his voice warm and rich, "I suppose we're offering floor s'mores now."

Stephanie felt her heart skip a beat at the sound of his laughter. "Maybe we should market it as a new holiday tradition," she quipped, bending down to scoop up the scattered marshmallows.

As they worked side by side to clean up the mess, Stephanie couldn't help but marvel at how natural it felt, working alongside Jack. His presence was comforting, steady.

"We make a pretty good team, don't we?" she murmured, almost to herself.

Jack paused, his gaze meeting hers with an intensity that made her breath catch. "We do," he agreed softly.

The moment was broken by a chorus of "awws" from the crowd. Tessa had curled up beneath a nearby table, looking entirely too pleased with herself.

"Don't think you're off the hook, missy," Stephanie said, wagging a finger at the unrepentant pup. "We've still got our eyes on you."

With the marshmallow mishap resolved, Stephanie turned her attention back to the guests. The air was thick with the aroma of cinnamon and vanilla, punctuated by the rich scent of cocoa. Laughter and the gentle clink of cups filled the bakery, creating a symphony of holiday cheer.

Stephanie's eyes scanned the bustling bakery, searching for any sign of their furry escapee. Suddenly, she caught a glimpse of glossy black fur nestled beneath the twinkling lights of the Christmas tree.

"Jack," she whispered, gently touching his arm. "Look."

There, curled up on a plush red tree skirt, lay Tessa. Her little chest rose and fell steadily, her mischievous energy finally spent.

Jack's lips curved into a soft smile. "Looks like our little troublemaker has finally run out of steam."

They approached quietly, careful not to startle the sleeping pup. Stephanie knelt down, her fingers gently stroking Tessa's silky ears. "She's actually pretty adorable when she's not causing chaos," she murmured.

Jack chuckled, the sound low and warm. "I suppose we should get her back to Cindy before she wakes up and decides to redecorate the tree."

As Jack scooped up the sleeping dachshund, Stephanie felt a surge of affection for both man and dog. Their eyes met over Tessa's sleeping form, and Stephanie's heart fluttered at the tenderness in Jack's gaze.

"We did it," she said softly, her voice filled with a mix of triumph and something deeper.

"We certainly did," Jack replied, his blue eyes twinkling. "Though I'm not sure if we're talking about catching Tessa or pulling off this amazing event."

Stephanie laughed, the sound light and joyous. "Both, I think."

They made their way through the crowd, stopping to hand Tessa over to a grateful Cindy. As they watched the woman cradle the sleeping pup, Stephanie felt a wave of contentment wash over her.

"You know," she said, turning to Jack, "I think this might be the best Christmas Eve I've had in years."

Jack's expression softened. "Me too, Stephanie. There's something special about this place... and the people in it."

Stephanie's cheeks warmed at his words, and she allowed herself a moment to simply take in the scene around them. The bakery glowed with warmth and cheer, filled with the sounds of laughter and the clinking of cocoa mugs. Everywhere she looked, she saw smiling faces and twinkling eyes.

"We really did it, didn't we?" she mused, more to herself than to Jack. "Look at how happy everyone is."

Jack nodded, his gaze sweeping across the room. "It's pretty incredible. You should be proud, Stephanie. This is all because of you and your amazing cookies."

Stephanie felt a rush of gratitude. "Not just me," she insisted, meeting his eyes. "We did this together, Jack. I couldn't have pulled it off without you."

Stephanie's heart swelled with warmth as she surveyed the room, filled with the cheerful chatter of her neighbors and friends. The scent of cinnamon and chocolate hung in the air, mingling with the fresh pine aroma from the Christmas tree.

"I think it's time for our final toast," Jack said softly, his blue eyes twinkling with mischief. "Shall we gather the troops?"

Stephanie nodded, a smile playing on her lips. "Let's do it."

They made their way to the center of the bakery, gently clinking spoons against their mugs to capture everyone's attention. The room gradually fell silent, all eyes turning towards them.

"Friends," Stephanie began, her voice filled with emotion, "Jack and I want to thank you all for coming tonight and making this event so special."

Jack chimed in, his usual reserve melting away. "We've been overwhelmed by your support and enthusiasm. This town truly embodies the spirit of Christmas."

Stephanie raised her mug of cocoa, the rich aroma wafting up. "So, let's raise our cups to Hollybrook, to new friendships, and to the magic of the season!"

The room erupted in a chorus of "Cheers!" as mugs clinked together. Stephanie took a sip of her cocoa, savoring the creamy sweetness. As she lowered her mug, she caught Jack's gaze, and a spark of understanding passed between them.

As the crowd began to disperse, Stephanie and Jack found themselves leaning against the bakery counter, watching as their guests bundled up and headed out into the crisp night air.

"I can't believe it's over," Stephanie murmured, a hint of wistfulness in her voice. "It feels like we've been planning this forever."

Jack nodded, his shoulder brushing against hers. "Time flies when you're having fun... and chasing mischievous dachshunds."

Stephanie laughed, the sound filling the now-quiet bakery. "Oh, Tessa. She certainly kept us on our toes."

"Just like someone else I know," Jack teased, his eyes soft as they met hers.

Stephanie felt a flutter in her chest, realizing how close they were standing. "Jack, I... I'm really glad you were here for this. For all of it."

He turned to face her fully, his expression serious but warm. "So am I, Stephanie. I never expected to find... this when I came to Hollybrook."

As the last guest waved goodbye and stepped out into the snowy night, Stephanie and Jack shared a quiet moment, their connection palpable in the twinkling lights of the bakery.

Stephanie's gaze lingered on the closed door for a moment before she turned to Jack, her eyes sparkling with determination. "Well, I suppose
we'd better get this place cleaned up," she said, clapping her hands together.

Jack nodded, rolling up his sleeves. "Where do we start, boss?"

Stephanie chuckled, her heart warming at his eagerness. "Let's tackle these tables first. I'll grab the cleaning supplies."

As Stephanie retrieved the cleaning caddy from beneath the counter, Jack began stacking plates and cups. They fell into an easy rhythm, moving around each other with a synchronized grace that surprised them both.

"You know," Stephanie said, wiping down a table with a damp cloth, "I never thought I'd say this, but I'm actually enjoying the clean-up process."

Jack raised an eyebrow, a smirk playing on his lips. "Oh? And why's that?"

Stephanie felt a blush creep up her cheeks. "Well, the company's not bad," she admitted, her voice soft.

Jack's smile widened as he gathered a handful of napkins. "I'd have to agree. Though I must say, I prefer your company when you're covered in flour and frosting."

Stephanie laughed, tossing her cleaning rag at him playfully. "Hey! I'll have you know I clean up quite nicely."

"Oh, I've noticed," Jack replied, his voice low and warm.

They continued working, the air between them charged with unspoken feelings. Stephanie found herself stealing glances at Jack, admiring the way his muscles moved beneath his shirt as he wiped down the windows.

As they packed away the remaining cookies, Stephanie couldn't help but feel a twinge of nostalgia. "It's a shame to see them go," she sighed, carefully placing a tray of gingerbread men into a storage container.

"We could always eat them ourselves," Jack suggested with a mischievous grin.

Stephanie giggled, shaking her head. "Don't tempt me. I've already eaten far too many sweets today."

"Nonsense," Jack replied, popping a small cookie into his mouth. "It's Christmas Eve. Calories don't count."

Stephanie rolled her eyes affectionately, but couldn't resist snagging a cookie for herself. The sweet, buttery flavor melted on her tongue, and she closed her eyes in bliss.

"See?" Jack said, his voice tinged with amusement. "Worth it."

As they finished the last of the cleaning, Stephanie glanced around the bakery, taking in the twinkling lights and the lingering scent of cinnamon and vanilla. Her heart swelled with pride and contentment.

"Ready to lock up?" Jack asked, jingling the keys.

Stephanie nodded, a bittersweet feeling washing over her. "Yeah, I think we're done here."

They moved towards the door, and Stephanie couldn't help but feel like this moment marked the end of something special and the beginning of something even more extraordinary.

As Jack turned the key in the lock, the soft click seemed to echo in the quiet night. Stephanie gazed up at him, her breath catching at the tender look in his blue eyes.

"So," she said, her voice barely above a whisper, "what now?"

Jack's hand found hers, his fingers intertwining with her own. The warmth of his touch sent a shiver down her spine.

"Now," he said, his voice low and full of promise, "we walk into our future together."

They stepped out into the crisp night air, the stars twinkling overhead like a blanket of diamonds. Stephanie's heart raced with excitement and anticipation for what lay ahead.

As they walked hand in hand down the snow-dusted sidewalk, Stephanie couldn't help but marvel at how perfectly their hands fit together, like two pieces of a puzzle finally united.

"You know," she said, her voice filled with wonder, "I never imagined that Sugar & Spice would bring me so much more than just a successful business."

Jack squeezed her hand gently. "Sometimes the sweetest things in life come when we least expect them."

Stephanie laughed softly, the sound carried away on the gentle winter breeze. "That was terribly cheesy, you know."

"What can I say?" Jack grinned, pulling her closer. "You bring out the sap in me."

As they continued their leisurely stroll through the twinkling streets of Hollybrook, Stephanie felt a sense of certainty settle over her. Whatever challenges lay ahead, she knew that with Jack by her side and the love of their community behind them, they could face anything.

The magic of Sugar & Spice, she realized, wasn't just in the delectable treats they created. It was in the connections they forged, the joy they spread, and the love that had blossomed between them.

Chapter 15

The soft glow of fairy lights twinkled overhead as Stephanie led Jack to a secluded nook in the corner of Sugar & Spice Bakery. The scent of cinnamon and freshly baked gingerbread lingered in the air, a comforting embrace that usually calmed her nerves. But tonight, her heart raced as she settled into a plush armchair, her fingers nervously tracing the intricate snowflake pattern on her flour-dusted apron.

Jack sat across from her, his piercing blue eyes softening as he reached for her hand. "Stephanie, what's on your mind? You've been quiet all evening."

She took a deep breath, the warmth from his touch spreading through her like hot cocoa on a cold winter's night. "Jack, I... I'm scared," she admitted, her voice barely above a whisper. "This job offer in New York, it's an amazing opportunity for you, but..."

Stephanie's gaze drifted to the bustling kitchen beyond, where the last batch of Christmas cookies cooled on the rack. The thought of losing Jack, of him returning to the fast-paced world he'd left behind, made her stomach churn like poorly mixed batter.

"I can't help but worry about what it means for us, for Sugar & Spice," she continued, her eyes meeting his once more. "This bakery, it's not just my livelihood, it's my heart and soul. And you... you've become such an important part of my life here in Hollybrook."

Jack leaned forward, his brow furrowed with concern. "Stephanie, I had no idea you were feeling this way. Tell me more."

She bit her lower lip, tasting the faint sweetness of the peppermint lip balm she'd applied earlier. "I'm afraid that if you go back to New York, you'll realize what you've been missing. The excitement, the culture, the endless possibilities. And then... then you might not want to come back to our little town anymore."

As she spoke, Stephanie's eyes welled up with tears, mirroring the twinkling lights above. She blinked them away, determined to express her fears fully. "And without you here, without your support and your love, I'm not sure I can keep Sugar & Spice going. It's been struggling lately, and I..."

Her voice trailed off as Jack squeezed her hand gently, his touch as reassuring as the warmth of a freshly baked loaf of bread. The muffled sounds of carolers outside drifted through the bakery, a bittersweet reminder of the joy and community spirit that filled Hollybrook during the holiday season.

Stephanie's heart ached at the thought of losing all of this – the bakery, the town, and most importantly, Jack. She looked up at him, her brown eyes wide with vulnerability, silently pleading for reassurance, for a promise that their story wouldn't end here, in this cozy corner of Sugar & Spice Bakery.

Jack gazed at Stephanie, the corners of his mouth turning up into a gentle smile. The scent of cinnamon and vanilla lingered in the air, wrapping around them like a comforting blanket.

"Stephanie," he said, his voice low and steady, "I turned down the job offer in New York."

Stephanie's lips parting in surprise. "You... you did?"

Jack nodded, reaching out to tuck a stray strand of chestnut hair behind her ear. "I realized something important. My true happiness isn't in the hustle and bustle of the city. It's right here, in Hollybrook, with you."

Stephanie's heart swelled, a warmth spreading through her chest. She leaned into his touch, savoring the roughness of his fingers against her cheek. "But Jack, your career..."

"My career brought me here," he interrupted gently. "And I'm grateful for that. But this town, this bakery, you... that's where my heart is now."

Stephanie bit her lip, her fingers absently tracing the pattern on her flour-dusted apron. "I've been having doubts too," she admitted. "About expanding Sugar & Spice into a franchise."

Jack raised an eyebrow, encouraging her to continue.

"It's just," Stephanie sighed, gesturing around the cozy bakery, "I love this. The personal connections, knowing our customers by name, being part of the community. I'm not sure I want to lose that."

Jack nodded, understanding filling his eyes. "You're the heart of this town, Stephanie. Your passion for baking, the way you bring people together... it's special."

Stephanie felt a blush creep up her cheeks, warmer than the heat from the ovens. "So, what do we do now?" she asked, her voice barely above a whisper.

Jack gazed at Stephanie, a soft smile playing on his lips. "You know, Stephanie, it's your unwavering Christmas spirit that first drew me to you," he said, his voice filled with warmth. "The way you light up this entire town with joy... it's magical."

Stephanie felt her cheeks flush, the cinnamon-scented air suddenly feeling warmer. "It's just who I am," she murmured, fiddling with a stray ribbon on her apron.

"And it's who I want to be with," Jack affirmed, reaching out to take her flour-dusted hands in his. "I want to be part of this world you've created here in Hollybrook."

The soft glow of twinkling lights reflected in Stephanie's eyes as she looked up at Jack. "Really? You don't miss the excitement of New York?"

Jack chuckled, the sound rich and comforting like hot cocoa on a cold day. "Excitement? Sure. But happiness? That's right here."

Stephanie squeezed his hands, her heart brimming with emotion. "What about your dreams, Jack? Your aspirations?"

"They've changed," he said simply. "I used to think success meant fancy restaurants and critical acclaim. But now..." He paused, glancing around the bakery, taking in the homey atmosphere and the lingering scent of freshly baked gingerbread. "Now I dream of quiet mornings, community potlucks, and stealing kisses over cups of your famous peppermint hot chocolate."

Stephanie couldn't help but laugh, the sound tinkling like sleigh bells. "That does sound pretty perfect," she admitted. "I've been thinking about my dreams too. And I realize, I don't need a big franchise or national recognition. I just want to make people happy, one cookie at a time."

Jack nodded, his eyes twinkling. "And you do that so well. Your double chocolate chip cookies alone could bring world peace."

"Oh, stop," Stephanie giggled, playfully swatting his arm. But as their laughter faded, a contented silence fell between them. Stephanie realized that this - the warmth, the love, the sense of belonging - was everything she'd ever wanted.

Stephanie's fingers traced the worn edges of the wooden table, feeling every dent and scratch that told the story of countless conversations shared over steaming mugs of cocoa and plates of fresh pastries. She looked up at Jack, her brown eyes searching his blue ones.

"We've come a long way, haven't we?" she said softly, her voice barely louder than the gentle crackling of the fireplace across the room.

Jack nodded, a small smile playing on his lips. "From New York critic to small-town taste-tester. It's been quite the journey."

Stephanie chuckled, but there was a hint of vulnerability in her voice as she continued, "There were times I wasn't sure we'd make it. Remember our first Christmas cookie bake-off?"

Jack groaned playfully, "How could I forget? I nearly burned down your kitchen trying to prove I could outbake you."

"And I was so stubborn, refusing to admit that your chocolate ganache was actually better than mine," Stephanie added, shaking her head at the memory.

As they reminisced, Stephanie felt a familiar tightness in her chest. She took a deep breath, inhaling the comforting scent of cinnamon and nutmeg that perpetually hung in the air of Sugar & Spice.

"Jack," she began, her voice wavering slightly, "I'm scared. What if... what if I lose all of this? The bakery, the town, you?" Her last word came out as barely a whisper.

Jack reached across the table, enveloping her flour-dusted hands in his. "Stephanie, look at me," he said gently but firmly. When she met his gaze, he continued, "We've faced burnt cookies, snowstorms, and even my disastrous attempt at making your grandmother's famous fruitcake. If we can survive that, we can face anything."

Stephanie couldn't help but giggle at the memory of Jack's fruitcake fiasco, feeling some of the tension leave her shoulders. "You're right," she admitted. "We make a pretty good team, don't we?"

"The best," Jack agreed, his thumb tracing soothing circles on the back of her hand. "Whatever comes our way, we'll face it together. Just like we always have."

As Stephanie looked into Jack's eyes, she saw not just love, but a steadfast determination that made her heart swell. In that moment, surrounded by the warmth of the bakery and the strength of their bond, she knew that together, they could overcome any obstacle life threw their way.

Stephanie took a deep breath, inhaling the comforting scent of cinnamon and vanilla that lingered in the air. She squeezed Jack's hand, drawing strength from his unwavering support.

"You know what, Jack? I think we need to tell Peter Hamilton thanks, but no thanks," Stephanie said, her voice growing stronger with each word. "Sugar & Spice isn't just a bakery; it's the heart of Hollybrook. I can't imagine turning it into some soulless franchise."

Jack's eyes lit up, a smile spreading across his face. "I couldn't agree more. The charm of this place, the way it brings the community together – that's something you can't replicate in a big city."

Stephanie nodded enthusiastically, her chestnut hair bobbing as she did. "Exactly! Remember last Christmas when old Mrs. Johnson's oven broke down? We baked her entire family's holiday dinner right here."

"And don't forget about the Great Gingerbread House Competition," Jack added, chuckling. "I've never seen so many adults get that excited over cookie architecture."

They both laughed, the sound mingling with the gentle tinkling of the bakery's bell as the last customer of the day left. Stephanie's gaze swept over the cozy space, taking in the twinkling fairy lights and the snow gently falling outside the frosted windows.

"Jack," she said softly, turning back to him. "I love you. And I love this town, with all its quirks and traditions. I can't imagine being anywhere else or with anyone else."

Jack's blue eyes softened, his thumb gently caressing Stephanie's hand. "I love you too, Stephanie. More than I ever thought possible. You and this town have shown me what really matters in life."

Stephanie felt her heart swell with emotion. "So, what do you say? Are you ready for more small-town adventures with me?"

"Absolutely," Jack replied without hesitation. "Who knows? Maybe next year we'll finally crack the code on your grandmother's secret eggnog recipe."

Stephanie giggled, her eyes sparkling with mirth and love. "Now that's an adventure I can't wait to embark on with you, Jack Carter."

As their laughter subsided, Stephanie felt a wave of contentment wash over her. She reached out, intertwining her fingers with Jack's. His hand was warm and strong, a perfect fit for hers. The scent of cinnamon and vanilla lingered in the air, wrapping around them like a comforting blanket.

"You know," Stephanie said, her voice barely above a whisper, "I never thought I'd find someone who understands me the way you do. Someone who sees the magic in a perfectly frosted cupcake or the joy in a child's face when they bite into their first gingerbread cookie."

Jack squeezed her hand gently. "And I never imagined I'd find someone who could make me appreciate the simple things in life again. You've shown me that there's more flavor in one of your homemade pies than in all the fancy restaurants I've ever reviewed."

Stephanie felt a blush creep up her cheeks. She gazed around the bakery, taking in the twinkling lights reflecting off the polished display cases, the soft glow of the vintage chandelier, and the warmth emanating from the ovens. This place, this moment—it was perfect.

"We make a pretty good team, don't we?" she mused, turning back to Jack.

He nodded, a smile playing on his lips. "The best. Sweet and savory, just like your famous chocolate-covered pretzels."

Stephanie laughed, the sound echoing through the empty bakery. "Well, Mr. Food Critic, I think we're ready to face whatever comes our way. Be it a rush of holiday orders or—"

"—or Mrs. Henderson's annual request for a life-sized gingerbread replica of her cat," Jack finished, his eyes twinkling with amusement.

They stood up together, still holding hands. Stephanie felt a surge of determination coursing through her veins. With Jack by her side, she knew they could handle anything life threw at them.

"Alright, partner," she said, giving his hand one last squeeze before releasing it to grab her apron. "Let's close up shop and head home. We've got a big day tomorrow, starting with perfecting that new cinnamon roll recipe."

Jack grinned, already moving to help her. "I wouldn't miss it for the world."

As they worked side by side, tidying up the bakery, Stephanie couldn't help but feel grateful for the path that had led them here. Together, they were ready to write the next chapter of their story in Hollybrook, one sweet moment at a time.

Chapter 16

The bell above the bakery door chimed merrily as Stephanie and Jack stepped inside, their cheeks flushed from the crisp winter air and eyes sparkling with joy. The warmth of Sugar & Spice enveloped them instantly, carrying with it the heavenly aroma of cinnamon, nutmeg, and freshly baked cookies.

"We did it, Jack!" Stephanie exclaimed, her voice barely audible above the cheerful din that filled the cozy space. She squeezed his hand, her heart swelling with pride and affection.

Jack's lips curved into a rare, genuine smile as he gazed down at her. "No, Stephanie. You did it. This is all you."

Stephanie's protest was drowned out by the enthusiastic applause that erupted as the townspeople noticed their arrival. The bakery was packed to the brim, with familiar faces beaming at them from every corner. Twinkling fairy lights cast a warm glow over the festive scene, highlighting the joy etched on each face.

"I can't believe how many people showed up," Stephanie whispered, her eyes wide with wonder as she took in the sight. The thought of her little bakery bringing so much happiness to Hollybrook made her chest tighten with emotion.

Barking Up The Wrong Bakery

Jack leaned in close, his breath tickling her ear. "Believe it. Your passion is contagious, Stephanie. You've given this town something truly special."

Stephanie felt a blush creep up her neck, and not just from the heat of the bakery. She was about to respond when Mrs. Johnson, the town's self-appointed social coordinator, bustled over with a plate piled high with gingerbread men.

"Stephanie, dear! These cookies are simply divine," she gushed, holding out the plate. "I must have the recipe for our next bake sale!"

Stephanie laughed, the sound mingling with the cheerful chatter around them. "I'd be happy to share it with you, Mrs. Johnson. Though I'm sure Jack here could describe the flavors better than I ever could."

Jack raised an eyebrow, a hint of his food critic persona peeking through. "Well, if you insist," he said, plucking a cookie from the plate with a flourish. "The ginger provides a warming kick, perfectly balanced by the molasses' rich sweetness. And the texture? Crisp edges giving way to a gloriously chewy center. Truly a masterpiece of holiday baking."

As Mrs. Johnson clapped in delight, Stephanie felt a surge of affection for Jack. Who would have thought the once-aloof critic would be standing in her small-town bakery, earnestly praising her humble gingerbread men?

The festivities continued around them, a joyful cacophony of laughter, clinking mugs of hot cocoa, and the occasional burst of off-key caroling. Stephanie soaked it all in, marveling at how her childhood dream of spreading happiness through baking had blossomed into this magical reality.

Stephanie squeezed Jack's hand, her heart brimming with gratitude. "Thank you all for coming," she said, her voice warm and sincere. "Your support means the world to us."

As they moved through the crowd, the scent of cinnamon and vanilla enveloped them. Stephanie paused to admire a group of children decorating sugar cookies, their faces dusted with colorful sprinkles.

"Look at their smiles," she whispered to Jack, her eyes twinkling. "This is what Christmas is all about."

Jack nodded, his usual reserve softening. "You've created something special here, Stephanie."

They continued their circuit, stopping to chat with Mr. Peterson about his grandchildren's visit and complimenting Sarah on her festive sweater. The bakery hummed with joy and laughter, strings of twinkling lights casting a warm glow over the scene.

Stephanie found herself by the window, watching snowflakes dance in the lamplight outside. She took a deep breath, overwhelmed by the love filling her little bakery.

"I never imagined it could be like this," she thought, her eyes misting slightly. Sugar & Spice had always been her dream, but seeing it become a cherished part of Hollybrook's Christmas tradition filled her with a pride and happiness she could barely contain.

Jack joined Stephanie by the window, his tall frame casting a gentle shadow. His piercing blue eyes, usually guarded, now shone with a warmth that matched the twinkling lights adorning the bakery. He gazed at the bustling scene before them, a soft smile playing on his lips.

"You know," he said, his voice low and thoughtful, "I've seen some of the most acclaimed restaurants in New York, but this..." He gestured to the joyful crowd. "This is something truly special."

Stephanie's heart swelled at his words. She looked up at him, noticing how the golden glow of the bakery softened his usually stern features. "Really? You think so?"

Before Jack could respond, Mrs. Hemingway, the town's librarian, approached them, her cheeks rosy from laughter and warmth. "Stephanie, dear! These gingerbread men are simply divine. They remind me of the ones my grandmother used to make."

Stephanie beamed, the scent of ginger and molasses wafting around them. "Oh, I'm so glad you like them! What was your grandmother's secret ingredient?"

As Mrs. Hemingway launched into a story about her grandmother's baking, Stephanie felt Jack's hand rest gently on the small of her back. She leaned into his touch, savoring the moment of connection amidst the festive chaos.

"And what about you, Jack?" Mrs. Hemingway asked, turning her twinkling eyes to him. "Do you have a favorite holiday treat?"

Jack cleared his throat, a hint of his old hesitancy creeping in. "Well, I've always been partial to a good fruit cake, actually."

Stephanie couldn't help but giggle. "Fruit cake? Mr. Sophisticated Food Critic likes fruit cake?"

Jack's eyes crinkled with amusement. "What can I say? It's a classic for a reason."

As they continued to chat and laugh with the townspeople, Stephanie marveled at how seamlessly Jack had become a part of this community. The once-aloof critic now stood beside her, genuinely engaged in conversations about family recipes and holiday traditions.

Stephanie gently tugged Jack's sleeve, guiding him towards a quiet corner of the bakery. The cheerful din of the celebration faded slightly as they found a moment of relative privacy near the twinkling Christmas tree.

"Can you believe we've come this far?" Stephanie asked, her warm brown eyes reflecting the soft glow of the fairy lights. She absently brushed a dusting of flour from her festive red sweater.

Jack's piercing blue eyes softened as he gazed at her. "It hasn't been an easy road," he admitted, his voice low and thoughtful. "Remember when I first walked into Sugar & Spice, ready to tear it apart in my review?"

Stephanie chuckled, the sound as sweet as the cinnamon rolls cooling on the nearby rack. "How could I forget? You looked like you'd bitten into a lemon instead of my lemon tart."

"In my defense," Jack said with a wry smile, "I was still in full-blown New York critic mode. I didn't realize what I was walking into."

Stephanie playfully swatted his arm. "You mean you didn't expect to fall head over heels for small-town charm and my irresistible baking skills?"

Jack caught her hand, his touch sending a warmth through her that rivaled the heat from the ovens. "Or for the baker herself," he murmured.

Stephanie felt a blush creep up her cheeks. She glanced around at the packed bakery, at the faces of friends and neighbors all aglow with holiday cheer. "We couldn't have done this without them, you know," she said softly. "The whole town rallied around us when we needed it most."

Jack nodded, his expression thoughtful. "I never understood the power of community until I came here. In New York, everything was a competition. But here..."

"Here, it's about lifting each other up," Stephanie finished for him. She squeezed his hand. "I'm so grateful for every person who believed in us, who pitched in when we were renovating, who spread the word about our Christmas cookie tasting."

Jack's eyes twinkled mischievously. "Even Mrs. Hawkins and her relentless campaign to perfect your snickerdoodle recipe?"

Stephanie laughed, the sound mingling with the cheerful notes of "Jingle Bell Rock" playing in the background. "Especially Mrs. Hawkins. Her persistence might drive me crazy sometimes, but her heart's in the right place."

They shared a moment of comfortable silence, watching the joyful scene before them. Stephanie felt a swell of emotion in her chest, overwhelmed by how far they'd come and how much love surrounded them.

Stephanie's fingers intertwined with Jack's, their hands fitting together perfectly like two pieces of a puzzle. The warmth of his touch sent a comforting tingle up her arm, grounding her in this perfect moment. She turned to face him, her brown eyes sparkling with unshed tears of joy.

"Jack," she whispered, her voice thick with emotion, "I never imagined Sugar & Spice could become this... this beacon of happiness for Hollybrook. And I certainly never dreamed I'd find someone like you to share it with."

Jack's eyes softened as he glanced at her, a gentle smile playing on his lips. "Stephanie," he said, his voice low and sincere, "you've not only transformed this bakery, but you've also transformed me. I promise to stand by your side through every batch of cookies and every challenge we face."

Stephanie's heart swelled with affection. She leaned in closer, inhaling the comforting scent of cinnamon and vanilla that seemed to cling to Jack now. "I love you," she murmured, "and I love our little bakery family."

Jack's thumb traced soothing circles on the back of her hand. "Speaking of family," he said, a hint of excitement creeping into his voice, "I've been thinking about some ideas to make Sugar & Spice even more special."

Stephanie's eyes lit up with curiosity. "Oh? Do tell, Mr. Former Food Critic," she teased gently.

"Well," Jack began, his eyes dancing with enthusiasm, "what if we started a monthly baking class for kids? We could teach them simple recipes, let them decorate cookies... it would be a great way to involve the community even more."

Stephanie gasped softly, her mind already racing with possibilities. "Jack, that's brilliant! We could even do themed classes for different holidays. Can you imagine tiny witches and wizards decorating Halloween cookies?"

They both chuckled at the image, their laughter mingling with the cheerful bustle of the bakery around them.

Stephanie's eyes drifted to the display case, where a single slice of their signature Christmas spice cake remained. "You know," she said, her voice warm with affection, "I think we've earned a little celebration of our own."

Jack followed her gaze and smiled, his blue eyes twinkling. "I couldn't agree more."

They made their way to the counter, hands still intertwined. Stephanie carefully lifted the slice onto a festive red and green plate, the rich aroma of nutmeg and cloves wafting up to tease their senses.

"Last piece," Jack observed, raising an eyebrow. "Are you sure you want to share?"

Stephanie playfully swatted his arm. "Don't you know by now? Everything's better when it's shared with you."

They found a quiet corner near the twinkling Christmas tree, where the soft glow of fairy lights cast a magical warmth over them. Stephanie took the first bite, closing her eyes in bliss as the flavors danced on her tongue.

"Mmm," she hummed. "I think this might be our best batch yet."

Jack took a bite and nodded in agreement. "It's perfect. Just like this moment."

As they savored the cake, the cheerful notes of "Jingle Bell Rock" filled the air. Stephanie's foot began tapping unconsciously to the beat, a spark of joy igniting in her chest.

Jack noticed and set down his fork, extending his hand with a playful bow. "May I have this dance, my Christmas cookie queen?"

Stephanie giggled, a light blush coloring her cheeks. "I thought you'd never ask, my culinary critic turned baker."

They joined the throng of townspeople on the makeshift dance floor, their bodies swaying in perfect harmony. Stephanie's chestnut hair, freed from its usual messy bun, swirled around her as Jack twirled her expertly.

"When did you learn to dance like this?" she asked, breathless with laughter and exertion.

Jack pulled her close, his voice low and warm in her ear. "Let's just say I've been practicing. I wanted to surprise you."

As they spun and laughed, surrounded by the joyful faces of their friends and neighbors, Stephanie felt a sense of completeness wash over her. This was more than just a successful business venture; it was the beginning of a beautiful life together, filled with love, laughter, and the sweet scent of freshly baked happiness.

The final notes of "White Christmas" faded away, and Stephanie found herself wrapped in Jack's arms, their foreheads touching as they swayed gently. The bakery, once filled with lively chatter and music, now settled into a contented hush. Only the soft clink of dishes being cleared and the muffled goodbyes of departing guests broke the silence.

Stephanie gazed up at Jack, her warm brown eyes shimmering with unshed tears of joy. "I can't believe this night," she whispered, her voice thick with emotion. "It's more than I ever dreamed possible."

Jack's piercing blue eyes softened as he tucked a stray strand of hair behind her ear. "You made it happen, Stephanie. Your passion, your dedication—it's infectious."

She shook her head, a gentle smile playing on her lips. "We made it happen, Jack. I couldn't have done this without you."

As they stood there, bathed in the warm glow of twinkling fairy lights, Stephanie's heart swelled with gratitude. She thought of all the challenges they'd faced, the late nights, the burnt batches, and the moments of doubt. Yet here they were, stronger than ever.

"You know," Jack began, his voice thoughtful, "when I first came to Hollybrook, I thought I was leaving everything behind. But really, I was finding everything I never knew I needed."

Stephanie squeezed his hand, her touch conveying all the words she couldn't express. "Sugar & Spice isn't just a bakery anymore," she mused. "It's become a home for so many people in this town."

Jack nodded, his eyes twinkling with determination. "And we'll keep it that way. A place where everyone can find a bit of warmth, love, and belonging—along with the best gingerbread in the state."

"Is that a promise, Mr. Food Critic?" Stephanie teased, her heart light with happiness.

"It's a guarantee, Ms. Master Baker," Jack replied, sealing his words with a tender kiss that tasted of cinnamon and new beginnings.

As they broke apart from their kiss, Stephanie's eyes sparkled with excitement. She gazed out the frosted window of Sugar & Spice, taking in the twinkling lights of Hollybrook's main street, now dusted with a fresh layer of snow.

"You know, Jack," she said, her voice soft but brimming with enthusiasm, "I can't help but feel like this is just the beginning of something truly magical."

Jack nodded, his arm settling comfortably around her waist. "I couldn't agree more. What's on that brilliant mind of yours?"

Stephanie's eyes lit up as she turned to face him. "Well, I was thinking... what if we expanded our holiday offerings? Maybe a winter wonderland themed high tea in January? Or Valentine's Day cookie decorating classes?"

Jack's lips curled into an admiring smile. "Always thinking ahead, aren't you? I love it."

"Can't help it," Stephanie laughed, the sound as warm and inviting as freshly baked bread. "Hollybrook has given us so much. I want to keep giving back."

As they stood there, the scent of cinnamon and vanilla still lingering in the air, Stephanie felt a surge of anticipation. The future stretched before them, as vast and full of possibility as a blank canvas—or in their case, an undecorated cookie.

"We could even look into catering for the spring festival," Jack suggested, his food critic mind already whirring with ideas.

Stephanie beamed, her heart swelling with affection. "See? This is why we make such a great team."

As snowflakes danced outside the window, Stephanie leaned into Jack's embrace, feeling truly at home. Whatever challenges lay ahead, she knew they'd face them together, creating sweet memories in Hollybrook one batch at a time.

Chapter 17

The Sugar & Spice Bakery glowed with warmth, twinkling lights reflecting off the polished glass display cases.

Stephanie's heart swelled with joy as she stood behind the counter, shoulder-to-shoulder with Jack. Their fingers brushed, sending a thrill through her despite the bustling activity around them.

"Welcome, everyone!" Stephanie called out, her voice brimming with enthusiasm. "Thank you all for coming to our Christmas celebration!"

Jack's deep voice chimed in, a hint of his former critic's eloquence shining through. "We're delighted to share this magical evening with you."

Stephanie snuck a glance at Jack, marveling at how natural he looked in this setting. His blue eyes sparkled with warmth, a far cry from the aloof food critic who had first walked into her bakery months ago.

As townspeople filed in, filling the air with cheerful chatter and the rustle of coats, Stephanie breathed in the mingled scents of cinnamon, nutmeg, and pine. She thought, 'This is everything I've ever dreamed of.'

"Stephanie, darling!" A familiar voice cut through the din.

Stephanie's face lit up as she spotted her mother weaving through the crowd, a tray of gingerbread cookies held aloft. "Mom! Oh, those smell heavenly!"

Maggie beamed, her eyes crinkling at the corners as she set the tray on the counter. "Fresh from the oven, just like you taught me." She turned to Jack, patting his arm affectionately. "And Jack, dear, you look right at home behind that counter."

Jack's cheeks flushed slightly, but his smile was genuine. "Thank you, Mrs. Fields. I'm learning from the best."

Stephanie felt a surge of pride, both for her mother's baking and for Jack's progress. She picked up a cookie, savoring the warmth seeping through her fingers. "Mom, these are perfect. You've outdone yourself."

Maggie's eyes sparkled with pride. "Oh, hush. This is your night, sweetheart. I couldn't be more proud of what you two have accomplished here."

As Stephanie bit into the cookie, the familiar flavors of her childhood Christmases flooded her senses. She closed her eyes briefly, overwhelmed by the moment.

Jack's hand found hers under the counter, giving it a gentle squeeze. When she opened her eyes, his gaze met hers, full of understanding and affection.

Stephanie thought, 'This is home. This is where I belong.'

The bell above the bakery door jingled merrily, and Stephanie's eyes widened as she saw Sam burst through, his curly blonde hair dusted with snowflakes. In his hands, he balanced an enormous cake, its surface a winter wonderland of white frosting and sparkling sugar.

"Make way for the pièce de résistance!" Sam called out, his voice ringing with laughter. He set the cake down on the counter with a flourish, revealing the elegantly piped message: "Congratulations Stephanie & Jack!"

Stephanie's heart swelled with emotion. "Oh, Sam," she breathed, "it's beautiful!"

Sam grinned, his eyes twinkling. "Well, I couldn't let you two have all the baking fun." He turned to Jack, playfully nudging him with an elbow. "So, Jack, I hear you've been conquering the mysterious world of measuring cups and mixer speeds. How's life as a baking novice treating you?"

Jack chuckled, running a hand through his dark hair. "Let's just say I have a newfound respect for anyone who can tell the difference between baking powder and baking soda."

Stephanie couldn't help but giggle, remembering Jack's first attempts at making scones. "He's actually become quite skilled with a rolling pin," she said, giving Jack an affectionate glance.

The bakery buzzed with warmth and joy, the air filled with the mingling scents of cinnamon, vanilla, and fresh coffee. Stephanie watched as her friends and neighbors laughed together, sharing stories and exchanging hugs. The soft glow of fairy lights strung across the ceiling cast a magical shimmer over everything.

'This is more than I ever dreamed,' Stephanie thought, her chest tight with happiness. 'A bakery full of love, laughter, and the spirit of Christmas.'

As Stephanie basked in the joyful atmosphere, she caught sight of her grandmother Martha weaving through the crowd, a mischievous glint in her eye. In her hand dangled a sprig of mistletoe, its white berries peeking out from glossy green leaves.

"Oh no," Stephanie whispered, her cheeks already warming. She nudged Jack gently. "Grandma alert. Twelve o'clock."

Jack turned, his blue eyes widening as he spotted Martha's approach. "Is that...?"

Before he could finish, Martha was upon them, her wrinkled face creased with a broad smile. "Well, well," she chirped, holding the mistletoe high above their heads. "Look what we have here!"

Stephanie felt her heart skip a beat as she met Jack's gaze. His lips quirked into a soft smile, a question in his eyes. She gave an almost imperceptible nod, her breath catching as he leaned in.

Their lips met in a sweet, tender kiss. Stephanie felt the world melt away, aware only of Jack's warmth, the softness of his lips, and the faint scent of cinnamon that clung to him. As they parted, the room erupted in applause and cheers.

'I could get used to this,' Stephanie thought, her face flushed with happiness and a touch of embarrassment.

As the applause died down, Stephanie noticed Cindy, Jack's sister, approaching. Her eyes shone with genuine warmth as she pulled Stephanie into a tight hug.

"Stephanie," Cindy said, her voice thick with emotion, "I can't thank you enough for everything you've done. Taking care of Tessa, being there for Jack... You've brought so much love and joy into his life."

Stephanie felt tears prick at her eyes. "Oh, Cindy," she replied, squeezing the other woman's hands. "Tessa's a sweetheart, and Jack... well, he's pretty special too."

Jack wrapped an arm around Stephanie's waist, his touch grounding her. "I'd say we both got lucky," he murmured, pressing a kiss to her temple.

As Cindy beamed at them, Stephanie felt a wave of contentment wash over her. This bakery, these people – this was home, in every sense of the word.

The warm glow of fairy lights twinkled off the festive baubles adorning Sugar & Spice Bakery as a line began to form in front of Stephanie and Jack. Stephanie's heart swelled with emotion as she watched her friends and neighbors approach, arms laden with carefully wrapped packages.

Mrs. Johnson, the town librarian, stepped forward first. "For you, dears," she said, her voice quavering slightly as she handed over a beautifully bound book. "It's filled with all our favorite recipes from the bakery over the years."

Stephanie's fingers traced the embossed cover, feeling the ridges of the golden letters spelling out "Sugar & Spice Memories." She blinked back tears, overwhelmed by the thoughtfulness.

"This is incredible," Jack said, his voice warm with genuine appreciation. "Thank you so much, Mrs. Johnson."

As Mrs. Johnson moved aside, Mr. Peterson, the retired woodworker, presented them with a delicately carved rolling pin. "For all your future baking adventures together," he said with a wink.

The gifts kept coming – hand-knitted potholders, a set of personalized aprons, even a collection of rare spices from around the world. Each item was infused with love and care, a testament to the bonds Stephanie and Jack had formed with the community.

"I never expected..." Stephanie whispered, her voice trailing off as she struggled to contain her emotions.

Jack squeezed her hand. "I know," he murmured. "It's overwhelming, isn't it? In the best possible way."

As the last gift was presented, Stephanie noticed her father, Henry, making his way to the center of the room. He cleared his throat, tapping a spoon against his glass to gather everyone's attention.

"Friends," Henry began, his usually gruff voice softened with emotion, "I'd like to propose a toast to my daughter Stephanie and to Jack." He paused, his gaze sweeping the room before settling on the couple. "When Stephanie first told me she wanted to open this bakery, I'll admit I had my doubts. But watching her pour her heart and soul into Sugar & Spice, seeing the joy it brings to our little town... well, I couldn't be prouder."

Stephanie felt Jack's arm tighten around her waist, anchoring her as waves of love and gratitude washed over her.

Henry continued, "And Jack, my boy, you've become such an integral part of not just the bakery, but our family. Your dedication, your willingness to dive headfirst into our crazy Christmas traditions – it's clear you two were meant to be."

"To Stephanie and Jack," Henry raised his glass high, "May your love continue to sweeten our lives, just like your delicious creations. And may your Christmas spirit shine bright, warming hearts for years to come."

The room echoed with a chorus of "To Stephanie and Jack!" as glasses clinked and smiles beamed from every corner. Stephanie turned to Jack, seeing her own joy and disbelief mirrored in his eyes.

"Merry Christmas, Jack," she whispered, leaning into his embrace.

"Merry Christmas, Stephanie," he replied softly, placing a gentle kiss on her forehead. "Here's to many more."

As the applause faded, Stephanie felt a gentle nudge from Jack. She took a deep breath, the scent of cinnamon and vanilla filling her lungs, and stepped forward. The room fell silent, expectant faces turned towards her. The twinkling Christmas lights cast a warm glow over the crowd, highlighting the love and support in their eyes.

"I-" Stephanie's voice caught, thick with emotion. She cleared her throat and tried again. "I can't begin to express how much your support means to us." Her gaze swept across the room, taking in familiar faces that had become like family. "Sugar & Spice isn't just a bakery. It's a dream come true, and it's all of you who've made it so special."

She gestured to the festive decorations and platters of treats. "Every time you walk through that door, every cookie you buy, every smile you share – you're not just customers. You're the heart of this community, and you've made Sugar & Spice a part of that heart."

Stephanie felt Jack's presence beside her, his warmth giving her strength. "Thank you for believing in us, for your patience when we were just starting out, and for making every day here feel like Christmas morning."

As Stephanie stepped back, her eyes shining with unshed tears, Jack took her hand. His touch sent a familiar tingle up her arm, and she marveled at how his presence still gave her butterflies.

Jack's steady voice filled the room. "When I first came to Hollybrook, I thought I was just passing through." He chuckled softly, and Stephanie remembered his initial reluctance to embrace small-town life. "But then I met Stephanie, tasted her incredible gingerbread, and realized I'd found something I never knew I was looking for."

His hands locked with Stephanie's, full of tenderness. "Stephanie, you've shown me what it means to truly be part of a community, to pour your heart into everything you do. Your passion is infectious, your kindness boundless." Jack's voice wavered slightly. "I can't wait to see what the future holds for us, both here in the bakery and in our life together."

Stephanie squeezed Jack's hand, her heart overflowing with love and joy. As she looked out at the sea of smiling faces, she knew that whatever challenges lay ahead, they'd face them together – surrounded by the warmth and support of their Hollybrook family.

The room erupted in thunderous applause, the sound of clapping hands mingling with joyous cheers and the tinkling of raised glasses. Stephanie's heart swelled with emotion as she looked around at the beaming faces of her friends and neighbors, their eyes twinkling like the Christmas lights strung across the bakery's ceiling.

"To love, friendship, and the magic of Christmas!" someone shouted, and the crowd echoed the sentiment enthusiastically.

Stephanie turned to Jack, her brown eyes sparkling with happiness. "I can't believe this is real," she whispered, her voice barely audible over the commotion.

Jack's lips curved into that soft smile she'd grown to adore. "Believe it," he murmured, reaching out to tuck a stray wisp of chestnut hair behind her ear. "May I have this dance, Ms. Fields?"

Stephanie giggled, feeling like a schoolgirl with her first crush. "Here? Now?"

"Why not?" Jack's eyes danced with mischief. "It's our bakery, after all."

Without waiting for an answer, Jack swept Stephanie into his arms, guiding her to the center of the room. The scent of cinnamon and vanilla enveloped them as they began to sway, the twinkling lights casting a warm glow on their faces.

"You know," Stephanie said, breathing in the comforting aroma of freshly baked cookies, "a year ago, I never would have imagined this."

Jack raised an eyebrow. "Dancing in a flour-dusted apron?"

Stephanie playfully swatted his shoulder. "No, you goof. This... us. The bakery thriving. It feels like a dream."

As they moved in slow circles, Stephanie marveled at how right it felt to be in Jack's arms. The once-aloof food critic had become her rock, her partner in both business and life. She rested her head on his chest, listening to the steady beat of his heart.

"If it's a dream," Jack murmured, his breath warm against her ear, "I never want to wake up."

As the last notes of the imaginary waltz faded away, Stephanie reluctantly pulled back from Jack's embrace. The bakery, once bustling with celebration, had quieted to a gentle hum of conversation. She caught sight of Mrs. Henderson, the town's librarian, gathering her coat.

"Oh, we should start saying goodnight," Stephanie whispered, her brown eyes widening with realization.

Jack nodded, his blue eyes twinkling. "Shall we, partner?"

Together, they made their way to the door where Mrs. Henderson stood. Stephanie enveloped the older woman in a warm hug, the scent of lavender and old books mingling with the bakery's sweet aromas.

"Thank you so much for coming, Mrs. Henderson," Stephanie said, her voice filled with genuine warmth. "Your support means the world to us."

"Oh, dearie," Mrs. Henderson replied, patting Stephanie's cheek. "I wouldn't have missed it for anything. You two have brought such joy to Hollybrook."

Jack, standing beside Stephanie, extended his hand. "We appreciate your kindness, Mrs. Henderson. I promise to return those cookbooks I borrowed... eventually."

The librarian chuckled, shaking his hand firmly. "See that you do, Mr. Carter. And maybe next time, I'll see some of your creations alongside Stephanie's?"

As Mrs. Henderson stepped out into the crisp night air, Stephanie turned to Jack, a teasing glint in her eye. "Cookbooks, huh? Planning on giving me a run for my money?"

Jack's cheeks reddened slightly. "Well, I thought I might try my hand at a few things. Can't let you have all the fun in the kitchen."

Stephanie's heart swelled with affection. The once-cynical food critic now wanted to bake alongside her. She squeezed his hand, marveling at how far they'd come.

As they continued to bid farewell to their guests, Stephanie felt a wave of gratitude wash over her. Each "thank you" and "goodnight" was infused with genuine appreciation for the community that had embraced them so wholeheartedly.

The last of the townspeople trickled out, carrying with them the lingering warmth of the evening. Stephanie watched as they disappeared down the snow-dusted street, their laughter echoing in the quiet night.

"Well," Jack said softly, closing the door behind the final guest. "That's a wrap."

Stephanie leaned against him, suddenly aware of the comfortable silence that enveloped them. The bakery, usually so full of life and noise, now felt like a cocoon of tranquility.

"It really is," she murmured, her eyes taking in the twinkling lights and the remnants of their celebration. "I can't believe it's over."

Stephanie and Jack made their way to a small table nestled in the corner of the bakery, the soft glow of fairy lights casting a warm hue over their faces. As they sat side by side, their fingers naturally intertwined, fitting together like pieces of a puzzle. The sweet aroma of cinnamon and vanilla lingered in the air, a comforting reminder of the evening's festivities.

Stephanie let out a contented sigh, her eyes sparkling as she gazed at Jack. "Can you believe how far we've come?" she asked, her voice barely above a whisper.

Jack's blue eyes met hers, a smile playing at the corners of his mouth. "From me critiquing your gingerbread to us running this place together? It's been quite the journey."

Stephanie chuckled softly, the sound like tinkling bells in the quiet bakery. "I still remember how terrified I was when you first walked in. The great Jack Carter, here to judge my humble creations."

"And now look at us," Jack mused, his thumb tracing gentle circles on the back of Stephanie's hand. "Partners in more ways than one."

As Stephanie leaned her head on Jack's shoulder, she caught sight of their reflection in the bakery window. The image before her - two people so clearly in love, surrounded by the warmth of Sugar & Spice - filled her heart with an indescribable joy.

"You know," she said thoughtfully, "I never imagined Hollybrook could feel even more like home than it already did. But with you here, it's like everything has fallen into place."

Jack pressed a soft kiss to the top of her head. "I never thought I'd find home in a small town bakery," he admitted. "But you've shown me that sometimes, the sweetest things in life come in the most unexpected packages."

Stephanie felt a warmth spread through her chest at his words. She lifted her head, meeting Jack's gaze with a mixture of love and excitement. "So, what do you think the future holds for us here in Hollybrook?"

Chapter 18

The aroma of warm spices filled the air as Stephanie rolled out the gingerbread dough, her fingers dusted with flour.

She glanced over at Jack, who was whisking the cinnamon roll filling with practiced ease. The early morning light filtered through the bakery's frosted windows, casting a soft glow on the kitchen.

"You know, for a former food critic, you're not half bad at this baking thing," Stephanie teased, her eyes twinkling with mischief.

Jack looked up from his bowl, a hint of a smile playing on his lips. "I'll take that as a compliment, coming from Hollybrook's very own baking queen."

Stephanie laughed, the sound as warm and inviting as the scent of gingerbread. She began cutting out cookie shapes, her movements quick and precise. "I still can't believe you traded in your fancy New York restaurants for our little bakery."

"Neither can I, sometimes," Jack admitted, his voice softening. "But there's something about the simplicity here that just feels right."

As Stephanie placed the cookies on a baking sheet, she couldn't help but wonder what other surprises Jack might have in store. There was still so much to learn about him, and the thought sent a little thrill through her.

"Well, we're glad to have you," she said, trying to keep her tone light. "Even if your cinnamon roll technique could use some work."

Jack raised an eyebrow, a challenge gleaming in his blue eyes. "Oh really? Care to demonstrate the proper method, Ms. Fields?"

Stephanie grinned, wiping her hands on her flour-dusted apron. "Watch and learn, Mr. Carter. This is how we do it in Hollybrook."

As she moved to Jack's side, their arms brushing, Stephanie felt a warmth that had nothing to do with the preheating ovens. She took a deep breath, inhaling the comforting scents of cinnamon and ginger, and began to show Jack the finer points of cinnamon roll assembly.

Stephanie's hands paused mid-roll as a spark of inspiration hit her. "You know, Jack, I've been thinking... We should add something new to our holiday menu. Something that really captures the spirit of Christmas in Hollybrook."

Jack's eyebrows lifted with interest, his blue eyes twinkling like the fairy lights adorning the bakery's windows. "I'm intrigued. What did you have in mind?"

Stephanie's warm brown eyes lit up as she began to gesticulate excitedly, a light dusting of flour falling from her hands. "Well, I was thinking... What if we combined the richness of chocolate with the coolness of peppermint? It's like... a sweet reminder of the first snowfall!"

Jack nodded thoughtfully, his critic's mind already analyzing flavor combinations. "Interesting... A chocolate base with a peppermint frosting, perhaps?"

"Exactly!" Stephanie exclaimed, her chestnut bun bobbing as she nodded enthusiastically. "We could make it into a cupcake. Ooh, and we could call it... 'Hollybrook's Peppermint Dream' or 'Frosty's Favorite'!"

Jack chuckled, his usually reserved demeanor softening. "How about 'Merry Mintmas'?"

Stephanie's laughter filled the bakery, warm and melodious. "Jack Carter, who knew you had such a way with words? I love it!"

Without missing a beat, Stephanie began to gather ingredients from the pantry, her petite frame moving with purpose. "Can you preheat the oven to 350, Jack? And maybe line the cupcake tins?"

"On it," Jack replied, his tall figure moving smoothly across the kitchen. As he worked, he couldn't help but marvel at Stephanie's enthusiasm. It was infectious, warming him from the inside out like a mug of hot cocoa on a cold winter's night.

Stephanie's mind raced with possibilities as she measured out flour and cocoa powder. 'This could be just what we need to bring even more Christmas cheer to Hollybrook,' she thought, a smile playing on her lips. 'And working on it with Jack... well, that's just the icing on the cupcake.'

Barking Up The Wrong Bakery

The rich aroma of chocolate and peppermint filled the bakery as Stephanie slid the cupcake tins into the oven. She dusted her flour-covered hands on her apron and turned to Jack with a bright smile.

"What do you say we take a little break while these bake?" she suggested, her warm brown eyes twinkling. "I could use some fresh air."

Jack nodded, a small smile tugging at the corners of his mouth. "Sounds perfect. I think we've earned it."

They stepped out into the crisp winter air, the bell above the bakery door jingling merrily. Stephanie's breath caught in her throat as she took in the sight before her. The town square was a winter wonderland, with twinkling lights adorning every tree and lamppost.

"Oh, Jack," she breathed, instinctively reaching for his hand. "Isn't it beautiful?"

Jack's fingers intertwined with hers, sending a warmth through Stephanie that had nothing to do with her cozy sweater. "It is," he agreed softly, his gaze fixed on her face rather than the decorations.

Stephanie felt a blush creep up her cheeks. "You know, I've lived in Hollybrook my whole life, but somehow, the Christmas lights never fail to take my breath away."

"I can see why," Jack murmured, his blue eyes reflecting the twinkling lights. "There's something magical about it."

They stood in comfortable silence for a moment, the only sound the soft crunch of snow beneath their feet. Stephanie's mind wandered to the man beside her, marveling at how his usually guarded expression had softened in the glow of the holiday lights.

"Jack," she said suddenly, turning to face him. "I'm so glad you're here. In Hollybrook, I mean. And... in the bakery."

Jack's grip on her hand tightened slightly. "So am I, Stephanie. More than I ever thought I would be."

The timer on Stephanie's phone chimed, breaking the spell. She laughed, a little breathlessly. "That's our cue. Ready to frost some cupcakes?"

Back inside the warm bakery, they set about their task with renewed energy. Stephanie carefully removed the perfectly baked cupcakes from the oven, the heavenly scent of chocolate and peppermint filling the air.

"They smell amazing," Jack commented, preparing the piping bags with creamy peppermint frosting.

Stephanie beamed, her heart swelling with pride. "Now for the fun part," she said, picking up a piping bag. "Watch and learn, Mr. Food Critic."

With practiced ease, Stephanie began piping delicate swirls onto each cupcake. Jack watched, mesmerized by her skill and the look of concentration on her face.

"Your turn," she said, handing him a piping bag. "Don't worry, I'll guide you."

Jack's larger hands engulfed Stephanie's as she showed him how to pipe the frosting. The simple act of decorating cupcakes suddenly felt incredibly intimate, and Stephanie found herself hyper-aware of Jack's presence beside her.

"Like this?" Jack asked, his voice low and close to her ear.

Stephanie swallowed hard, willing her racing heart to slow. "Perfect," she managed to say. "You're a natural."

As they continued to frost the cupcakes side by side, Stephanie couldn't help but think that maybe, just maybe, they were creating something even sweeter than cupcakes in this little bakery.

As Stephanie piped the last swirl of peppermint frosting onto a cupcake, the cheerful jingle of the bakery's bell announced the arrival of customers. The door swung open, letting in a gust of crisp winter air and the excited chatter of voices.

"Welcome to Sugar & Spice!" Stephanie called out warmly, setting down her piping bag and wiping her hands on her flour-dusted apron. She glanced at Jack, who was already moving towards the display case with a tray of their freshly decorated cupcakes.

A group of bundled-up townspeople filed in, their cheeks rosy from the cold and eyes bright with anticipation. Stephanie recognized Mrs. Thornberry, the town librarian, among them.

"Stephanie, dear! It smells absolutely divine in here," Mrs. Thornberry exclaimed, unwinding her scarf. "What heavenly concoction have you dreamed up today?"

Jack stepped forward, his usual reserved demeanor softening as he addressed the group. "We've just finished a new creation," he said, his voice carrying a hint of pride. "Peppermint chocolate cupcakes. Would you like to be our first taste-testers?"

Barking Up The Wrong Bakery

Stephanie's heart fluttered at Jack's use of 'we'. She watched as he carefully arranged the cupcakes on a festive platter, his movements precise and graceful.

"Oh, how lovely!" Mrs. Thornberry clapped her hands in delight. "We'd be honored!"

As Jack offered the platter around, Stephanie found herself holding her breath. These cupcakes represented more than just a new recipe; they were a symbol of her growing partnership with Jack, both in and out of the kitchen.

The first bite was met with a chorus of appreciative murmurs and wide-eyed looks of pleasure. Mrs. Thornberry closed her eyes, savoring the flavor. "My word, Stephanie and Jack, you've outdone yourselves! The chocolate is so rich, and that hint of peppermint is just perfect for the season."

Another customer chimed in, "And the frosting! So light and creamy. It's like Christmas in every bite!"

Stephanie felt a warm glow of satisfaction spread through her chest. She caught Jack's eye across the room, and they shared a silent moment of triumph. His usually stoic face broke into a rare, genuine smile that made Stephanie's knees go weak.

"We make a pretty good team, don't we?" Stephanie said softly as Jack returned to her side.

He nodded, his blue eyes twinkling. "Indeed we do, Miss Fields. Indeed we do."

The bell above the door chimed merrily as another group of customers bustled in, bringing with them a gust of crisp winter air and the faint jingle of distant sleigh bells. Stephanie inhaled deeply, savoring the mingled scents of cinnamon, gingerbread, and peppermint that perfumed the bakery.

"Welcome to Sugar & Spice!" she called out cheerfully, her hands dusted with flour as she kneaded dough for her famous Christmas star cookies.

An elderly couple approached the counter, their eyes twinkling with holiday spirit. "Oh, Stephanie dear," the woman said, "your bakery smells just like my grandmother's kitchen on Christmas Eve!"

Stephanie beamed, wiping her hands on her festive apron. "That's the best compliment I could ask for, Mrs. Henderson. What can I get for you today?"

As she chatted with the Hendersons about their family's tradition of leaving cookies for Santa, Stephanie couldn't help but steal glances at Jack. He was carefully boxing up an order of gingerbread men, his strong hands moving with surprising gentleness.

"Your turn at the register," Jack murmured as he passed by, his shoulder brushing hers. The brief contact sent a shiver down Stephanie's spine that had nothing to do with the December chill.

"Right," Stephanie nodded, trying to ignore the flutter in her stomach. She turned her attention to the growing line of customers, each one eager to share their own holiday stories as they selected their treats.

"Remember," she thought to herself, wrapping a loaf of cranberry bread, "focus on the bakery. This is what Christmas is all about – spreading joy through the perfect treat."

But as Jack's rich laugh echoed from across the room, Stephanie couldn't help but wonder if perhaps this Christmas held the promise of a different kind of sweetness.

As the last customer left, the cheerful jingle of the bell above the door faded into silence. Stephanie exhaled deeply, her shoulders relaxing as she surveyed the now-empty bakery. The scent of cinnamon and vanilla still lingered in the air, a comforting reminder of the day's successes.

"What a day," she sighed, reaching for a cloth to wipe down the counter. "I think we broke our sales record."

Jack nodded, already at the sink with his sleeves rolled up. "Your peppermint chocolate cupcakes were a hit," he said, a hint of pride in his voice. "I told you they'd be perfect."

Stephanie felt a warm glow in her chest at his words. As she moved around the bakery, collecting stray napkins and straightening chairs, she found herself stealing glances at Jack. His tall frame was bent over the sink, hands buried in soapy water as he tackled the mountain of dishes.

"You know," she said, pausing in her work, "I never thought I'd say this, but I'm actually enjoying closing time now."

Jack looked up, a questioning eyebrow raised. "Oh? And why's that?"

Stephanie felt her cheeks flush. "Well, it's... peaceful. And the company's not bad either."

A small smile tugged at the corner of Jack's mouth. "High praise indeed, coming from Hollybrook's queen of Christmas cheer."

Barking Up The Wrong Bakery

They fell into a comfortable rhythm, moving around each other with an ease that felt both new and familiar. Stephanie hummed softly as she swept, the tune of "Silver Bells" filling the quiet bakery.

"This reminds me of my first job," Jack said suddenly, breaking the silence. "I was a dishwasher at a diner in New York. It was chaos most of the time, but closing... closing was always my favorite part of the shift."

Stephanie paused, leaning on her broom. "Really? I wouldn't have pegged the famous food critic for a dishwasher."

Jack chuckled, the sound warming Stephanie more than any oven could. "We all start somewhere. Besides, it taught me to appreciate the behind-the-scenes work that goes into a good meal. Or in our case, a good pastry."

As they finished cleaning, Stephanie couldn't help but feel a sense of contentment wash over her. This bakery had always been her dream, but sharing it with Jack... that was something she'd never expected.

"Ready to lock up?" Jack asked, holding out her coat.

Stephanie nodded, slipping into the warmth of the wool. As they stepped outside, the cold air nipped at her cheeks, but she barely noticed. Her hand found Jack's, their fingers intertwining naturally.

The town square was a vision of holiday magic. Twinkling lights adorned every tree and lamppost, casting a soft glow over the freshly fallen snow. Stephanie's breath caught in her throat at the beauty of it all.

"It's like something out of a Christmas card," she whispered, squeezing Jack's hand.

He squeezed back, "It's perfect," he agreed, but Stephanie had a feeling he wasn't just talking about the scenery.

Stephanie felt a lump form in her throat as she gazed up at Jack. The twinkling lights cast a soft glow on his face, highlighting the warmth in
his eyes. She marveled at how far they'd come since he first walked into Sugar & Spice, his critic's notebook in hand.

"You know," she began, her voice soft with emotion, "I never imagined when I opened this bakery that I'd find... well, this." She gestured between them, a smile tugging at her lips.

Jack's eyebrows quirked up, a playful glint in his eye. "What, flour in your hair every day?"

Stephanie laughed, the sound carrying on the crisp night air. "No, you goof. This partnership. This... us."

Jack's expression softened, and he tugged her closer, wrapping an arm around her shoulders. "I know what you mean. When I left New York, I thought I was just looking for a quieter life. I never expected to find a home."

The word 'home' settled warmly in Stephanie's chest. She leaned into Jack's embrace, breathing in the comforting scent of cinnamon and vanilla that clung to his clothes.

"Hollybrook's been good to us," she murmured, her gaze sweeping over the festive town square.

"It has," Jack agreed. "But you know what's been even better?" He paused, waiting until Stephanie looked up at him. "You. Your passion, your kindness... you've reminded me why I fell in love with food in the first place."

Stephanie felt a blush creep up her cheeks, and not just from the cold. "Well, Mr. Food Critic, I'd say you've added some pretty special ingredients to my life too."

They shared a quiet laugh, their breath mingling in the frosty air. As they turned to walk home, Stephanie felt a familiar thrill of excitement. Tomorrow would bring new recipes to try, new customers to meet, new memories to make.

"So," Jack said, a mischievous tone in his voice, "what do you think about trying that peppermint mocha croissant idea tomorrow?"

Stephanie's eyes lit up. "Oh, that could be amazing! We could drizzle them with dark chocolate and..."

As they walked, trading ideas and dreams, Stephanie knew that whatever challenges lay ahead, they'd face them together – with a dash of sugar, a pinch of spice, and a whole lot of love.

Soft snowflakes began to fall as Stephanie and Jack made their way down the lamp-lit street, their footsteps crunching in perfect harmony on the freshly fallen snow. The twinkling lights from the storefronts cast a warm glow on their faces, illuminating Stephanie's rosy cheeks and the sparkle in Jack's blue eyes.

"You know," Stephanie said, her voice barely above a whisper, "I never thought I'd be this happy during the holiday rush. Usually, I'm so stressed I can barely enjoy the season."

Barking Up The Wrong Bakery

Jack squeezed her hand gently. "That's because you've always done it alone. Now you've got me to share the load... and the spatula."

Stephanie laughed, the sound like tinkling bells in the quiet night. "And the flour fights, apparently."

"Hey, you started that one," Jack protested with a grin.

As they walked, Stephanie breathed in deeply, savoring the crisp winter air mingled with the lingering scents of cinnamon and sugar that seemed to follow them everywhere. She glanced at Jack, marveling at how his presence made everything feel warmer, cozier, more... right.

"Jack?" she said softly.

"Hmm?"

"Thank you for choosing Hollybrook. For choosing... us."

Jack stopped, turning to face her. His expression was tender as he cupped her face with his free hand. "Best decision I ever made," he murmured, before leaning in for a sweet, unhurried kiss that tasted of peppermint and promises.

As they resumed their walk home, hand in hand, Stephanie's heart felt as light as the snowflakes dancing around them. The magic of Christmas, the joy of baking, and the warmth of true love – she had it all, right here in this perfect moment.

About the Author

Ladies and gentlemen, step right up to "Where the Magic Happens" - a literary circus that'll make your bookshelf do backflips!
Meet Patti, the ringmaster of this wordy wonderland! She's not just an Executive Producer; she's a word-wrangling wizard, conjuring up an animated TV series based on "ELLIOT FINDS A HOME." It's the tail-wagging tale of a thumbs-up pup and his silent sidekick, proving that you don't need words when you've got opposable digits and a heart of gold!

Hold onto your bestseller lists, folks! This Polygon Entertainment superstar has hit the USA TODAY jackpot and Amazon's #1 spot more times than a cat has lives. With 7 dozen books under her belt, she's got more genres than a chameleon has colors. From Urban Fantasy to Horror, she's been spinning yarns longer than your grandma's knitting needles!

But wait, there's more! Patti's life is like a celebrity bingo card:

She rocked "Romper Room" at 4, probably making the other kids look like amateur rompers.

She rubbed elbows with Captain Kangaroo and Mr. Green Jeans. (No word on whether the jeans were actually green.)

She shared a train ride and a sandwich with Sidney Poitier. Talk about a meal ticket to stardom!

Barking Up The Wrong Bakery

She high-fived President Nixon at the circus. Who knew the circus could get any more political?

She went to school with David Copperfield. We assume she didn't disappear during attendance.

She roller-skated with pre-famous John Travolta. Grease lightning, indeed!

She sipped cocoa with Abe Vigoda. Fish never tasted so sweet!

When she's not busy being a literary legend, Patti's juggling roles faster than a circus performer. Teacher, grandma, furparent - she does it all with a smile that could light up a haunted house.

Speaking of haunted houses, meet the "Queen of Halloween" herself! This Wiccan High Priestess is stirring up stories spookier than a skeleton's dance moves. Her books are flying off the shelves faster than witches on broomsticks, so follow her on social media or risk missing out on the hocus-pocus!

So, come one, come all, to Patti's phantasmagorical world of words! It's more exciting than a roller coaster, more magical than a rabbit in a hat, and more diverse than a box of assorted chocolates. Don't be shy - step into the spotlight and join the literary party where the pages turn themselves and the stories never end!

www.ingramcontent.com/pod-product-compliance
Lightning Source LLC
LaVergne TN
LVHW092048060526
838201LV00047B/1286